Quality Street

A COMEDY IN FOUR ACTS

by J. M. Barrie

This Acting Edition is published
by permission of
Charles Scribner's Sons

SAMUEL FRENCH

25 WEST 45TH ST.   NEW YORK 19

7623 SUNSET BLVD. HOLLYWOOD 46

LONDON   TORONTO

QUALITY STREET

Copyright, 1918, by J. M. Barrie

Copyright, 1946 (in renewal), by Lady Cynthia Asquith
Peter L. Davies and Barclay's Bank, Ltd.

ALL RIGHTS RESERVED

PRINTED IN U. S. A.

QUALITY STREET

STORY OF THE PLAY

(6 Males; 9 Females)

Quality Street is a cup of exquisite comic delight. Set in England, about 1800, it is alive with elegant humor and wit. There are several maiden women in the action, some of them a bit sour and curiously officious. But the one named Phœbe, with the plain face, is a sparkling lass whose heart flutters for a bachelor by the name of Valentine, who is expected on a visit. Sadly we learn, Valentine, has come back not to propose to Miss Phœbe but to announce his enlistment in the Napoleonic wars. And Phœbe, deserted to the glee of the gossiping women, is left with nothing to cherish but a kiss in the rain. Valentine returns ten years later to find that Phœbe and her sister have met economic misfortune by teaching a primary school. Rejuvenated by his return, Phœbe in a carefree moment discards her prim clothes and expression, and becomes a gay young girl, extravagant with her smiles, as well as with her dances at the military balls. The transformation is so complete that Phœbe is mistaken for a fictitious niece. The deception increases the merriment and produces many sudden changes of plot. Valentine discovers his love for Phœbe, and then fortunately discovers the precarious plot in time to save it from the mischievous women. Surely this is one of the most endearing and enduring of all comedies.

QUALITY STREET

Played for the first time in England at the Vaudeville Theatre, London, on September 17th, 1902.

CHARACTERS

VALENTINE BROWN	*Mr. Seymour Hicks.*
ENSIGN BLADES	*Mr. A. Vane-Tempest.*
LIEUT. SPICER	*Mr. Stanley Brett.*
RECRUITING SERGEANT	*Mr. George Shelton.*
A WATERLOO VETERAN	*Mr. Charles Daly.*
MASTER ARTHUR WELLESLEY THOMSON	*Master George Hersee.*
MISS SUSAN THROSSEL	*Miss Marion Terry.*
MISS WILLOUGHBY	*Miss Henrietta Watson.*
MISS FANNY WILLOUGHBY	*Miss Irene Rooke.*
MISS HENRIETTA TURNBULL	*Miss Constance Hyem.*
MISS CHARLOTTE PARRATT	*Miss May Taverner.*
PATTY (the maid)	*Miss Rosina Filippi.*
ISABELLA (a Schoolgirl)	*Miss Winifred Hall.*
HARRIET	*Miss Edith Heslewood.*
MISS PHŒBE THROSSEL	*Miss Ellaline Terriss.*

Officers. Ladies. School-children. A Lamplighter. And others.

SYNOPSIS OF SCENES

ACTS I, II AND IV

SCENE.—The Blue and White room in the house of Miss Susan and Miss Phœbe in Quality Street.

ACT III

SCENE.—A Tent Pavilion, used as a card and retiring-room at the Officers' Ball.

Ten years elapse between Acts I and II.
One week between Acts II and III.
Two days between Acts III and IV.

The SCENE is in England during the time of the Napoleonic Wars.

QUALITY STREET

Produced by Charles Frohman at the Knickerbocker Theatre, New York, November 11th, 1901.

CAST

PHOEBE THROSSELL	*Maude Adams*
MAJOR LINKWATER	*R. Payton Carter*
LIEUT. SPICER	*George Irving*
AN OLD SOLDIER	*Charles Martin*
MASTER TOMSON	*Fred Santley*
FANNY WILLOUGHBY	*Sarah Converse*
HENRIETTA TURNBULL	*Sara Perry*
VALENTINE BROWN	*Sydney Brough*
ENSIGN BLADES	*William Lewers*
MAJOR BUBB	*Frederick Spencer*
RECRUITING SERGT.	*Joseph Francoeur*
SUSAN THROSSELL	*Helen Lowell*
MISS WILLOUGHBY	*Ida Waterman*
PATTY	*Marion Abbott*

Staged by Joseph Humphreys. Settings by Edward G. Unitt.

5

Quality Street

ACT ONE

TIME.—*It is early afternoon in winter.*

SCENE.—*The blue and white room in the house of* MISS SUSAN *and* MISS PHŒBE *in Quality Street.*

An old-fashioned bay window—not a bow window —at the back commands a view of an old-fashioned street in a small English town in the beginning of the nineteenth century. The houses across the street are quaint and formal. Snow is falling and the roofs, so far as any are seen, are white with it. Snow falls at the beginning of the Act and again towards the close. The room is on the ground floor so that people passing in the street are visible to the audience. The room is pretty and very prim and feminine, suggesting an apartment seldom profaned by the foot of man. Tremendous care has been taken to have chair covers, book covers. cloths of all sorts either blue or white or both.

There are two couches, or settees, at R.C. *and* L.C. *respectively. Up stage* R., *below the bay, is an old-fashioned spinet and stool. The fire is in the* L. *wall. It is burning, and there is a kettle simmering on the hob.*

Between the fire and the settee, a chair with arms. Below the fire, a low stool. Down L. *a door to a bedroom.*

At the R. *wall, somewhat down stage, a large bureau desk, with leaded glass doors above and drawers be-*

6

low. Above this, a door to the hall, and the stairs. The remaining furniture, etc., is described in the Property Plot.

The CURTAIN *rises on* MISS SUSAN, MISS WILLOUGHBY, MISS HENRIETTA TURNBULL *and* MISS FANNY WILLOUGHBY, *all sitting. The first three are knitting or sewing, while* FANNY, *on the stool* L., *reads to them from a library book.* SUSAN *and* MISS WILLOUGHBY *are about thirty, which in those days was considered a hopelessly old-maidish time of life, but there is nothing about them to suggest the conventional old maid of the stage, except that* MISS WILLOUGHBY *is a little formidable. Both are refined ladies, and* SUSAN *who is timid, is particularly gentle and lovable.* HEN-RIETTA *and* FANNY *are sweet and prim and twenty. All are prettily dressed according to the period.* SUSAN *and* MISS WILLOUGHBY *wear white caps. The others are without headgear.* FANNY *has curls, but not a great show of them.*

The positions at the rise of the CURTAIN *are:*

SUSAN: *Sitting at the* L. *end of the settee* R.C.
MISS WILLOUGHBY: *Sitting* C. *of the settee* L.C.
HENRIETTA: *Sitting on the chair* L. *of the settee* **L.C.**
FANNY: *Sitting on the stool down* L.

None of them shows any oddities of appearance or gesture. The knitting goes on tranquilly while FANNY *reads.*

FANNY. "And so the day passed and evening came, black, mysterious and ghost-like. The wind moaned unceasingly like a shivering spirit and the vegetation rustled uneasy as if something weird and terrifying were about to happen. *(The clock chimes four.)* "Suddenly out of the darkness there emerged—"

HENRIETTA. A man!

FANNY. Yes.

MISS WILLOUGHBY. No! No!

(All knit more quickly. There must be no exaggeration or attempt to make broad effects. FANNY says the last word tremulously, but without looking up. The listeners tremble slightly, but do not look up. All, however, knit more quickly. They should always behave as refined ladies, and never as comic figures.)

FANNY. "The unhappy Camilla was standing lost in reverie when without pausing to advertise her of his intentions, he took both her hands in his—" *(By this time the knitting has stopped. All look horrified out front and are listening as if mesmerized.)* "— Slowly he gathered her in his arms—and rained hot, burning—"

HENRIETTA. Kisses!

FANNY. Yes.

MISS WILLOUGHBY *(rising)*. Sister!

FANNY *(greedily)*. "—on eyes, mouth, nose, ears—"

MISS WILLOUGHBY *(crossing down L.—sternly)*. Stop! *(She puts her hand on FANNY's mouth. Short gasps from the others. MISS WILLOUGHBY moves to below the R. end of the settee L.C.)* Miss Susan—I am indeed surprised you should bring such an amazing indelicate tale from the library. *(She sits.)*

(HENRIETTA goes on her knees by FANNY to read.)

SUSAN *(rising, leaving her work on the seat. Crushed and meek)*. Miss Willoughby, I deeply regret. *(Going to FANNY—who is reading quietly to herself.)* Oh, Fanny! *(She holds out her hand for the book. FANNY is reluctant. HENRIETTA, rising, returns to her chair.)* If you please, my dear! *(She takes the book and goes R. to the spinet.)*

MISS WILLOUGHBY. I thank you.

(SUSAN, *at the spinet, peeps slyly at the end of the book. In the pause a* RECRUITING SERGEANT *passes the window with two open-mouth* YOKELS *from* L. *to* R., *to whom he is evidently discoursing on the glories of war.*)

FANNY. Miss Susan is looking at the end.

(SUSAN *closes the book guiltily and comes down* L. *of the* R. *settee.*)

SUSAN *(apologetically).* Forgive my partiality for romance, Mary. I fear 'tis the mark of an old maid.

MISS WILLOUGHBY. Susan! That word!

SUSAN *(sweetly).* 'Tis what I am! *(She sits, as before.)* And you also, Mary, my dear.

FANNY *(rising to defend her sister).* Miss Susan, I protest—

MISS WILLOUGHBY *(woefully, but sternly truthful).* Nay, sister, 'tis true. We are known everywhere now. Susan, *you* and I, as the old maids of Quality Street.

(*General discomfort.* FANNY *sympathising, sits* L. *of* MISS WILLOUGHBY *and puts her hand on her sister's knee.*)

SUSAN *(brightly).* I am happy, Phœbe will not be an old maid.

HENRIETTA *(agitated).* Do you refer, Miss Susan, to Mr. V. B.?

(*All work quickly, and look at one another knowingly.*)

SUSAN. Phœbe of the Ringlets, as he has called her.

FANNY. Other females besides Miss Phœbe have ringlets.

SUSAN. But you and Miss Henrietta have to employ papers, my dear. *(Proudly.)* Phœbe never!

MISS WILLOUGHBY. I, do not approve of Miss Phœbe at all.

SUSAN. Mary, had Phœbe been dying you would have called her an angel, and that is ever the way. 'Tis all jealousy to the bride and good wishes to the corpse. *(A* POSTMAN *crosses the street* R. *to* L. *The ladies have risen indignantly, putting their work in their bags. Rising.)* My love. I beg your pardon.

MISS WILLOUGHBY *(moving down a little* L.C.*)*. With your permission, Miss Susan, I shall put on my tippet.

(She sails into the bedroom L.—*followed by* HEN-RIETTA, *who checks at the door, listening to the following conversation.)*

FANNY *(moving towards* SUSAN, *shyly)*. A bride! Miss Susan, do you mean that V. B. has declared?

*(*PHŒBE *is seen to cross, outside the window,* L. *to* R.*)*

SUSAN *(joyously)*. Fanny, I expect it hourly. *(A* CLERGYMAN *and a* LADY *cross the street* R. *to* L. FANNY *almost breaks down with a little cry, then exits* L., *preceded by* HENRIETTA. SUSAN *watches* FANNY *off, goes up and gets the book from the spinet, crosses to the settee* L.C., *sits, and reads.)* Oh! Oh!

PHŒBE *(off* R.*)*. Susan! Susan!

*(*SUSAN *hides the book under a cushion. Enter* PHŒBE R., *to down* R.C., *leaving the door open. She is twenty —her ringlets are much in evidence—she wears out-door dress of the period—and bonnet. She looks happy and excited.* SUSAN *rises, crosses* R., *and closes the door.)*

SUSAN *(turning to* PHŒBE *who has crossed to the settee* L.C.*)*. Phœbe! The carpet! Your pattens! *(*PHŒBE *sits* L.C. *on the settee and takes her pattens off. Re-*

turning to c.) Careful! (PHŒBE *goes to the fireplace, puts the pattens down and turns—*SUSAN *crosses to* L.C.) You seem strangely excited!

(The snow ceases.)

PHŒBE *(at the fireplace, back to it—her eyes agleam).* Susan, I have met a certain individual.

SUSAN *(agitated).* V. B.? (PHŒBE *nods in assent to the question in* SUSAN'S *face.)* My dear, you are trembling.

PHŒBE *(putting her hand to her heart).* No! Oh, no!

SUSAN. You have put your hand to your heart.

PHŒBE *(dropping her hand).* Did I? *(Implying awful things, she goes toward her.)* Sister! (SUSAN *points to the bedroom door* L., *signifying caution.* PHŒBE *looks at the door three times, turning between each to* SUSAN, *whispering the ladies' names.* PHŒBE *crosses down* R.C., *taking* SUSAN *across with her.)* Sister!

SUSAN. My love, has he offered?

PHŒBE (R.C., *appalled).* Oh, Susan!

(Enter MISS WILLOUGHBY L., *partly cloaked.)*

MISS WILLOUGHBY *(at* L.C.). How do you do, Miss Phœbe? *(Curtsy.* PHŒBE *curtsys and, crossing up* R.C., *takes off her hat and coat, which she puts on the spinet. Portentously.)* Susan, I have no wish to alarm you— but I am of opinion that there is a man in the house. (SUSAN *sits on the settee down* R.C.) I suddenly felt it while putting on my bonnet.

SUSAN. You mean—a follower—in the kitchen? (MISS WILLOUGHBY *nods assent and moves up,* R. *of the settee* L. PHŒBE *looks at* MISS WILLOUGHBY, *then at* SUSAN. SUSAN *rises, crosses to the fireplace and rings the bell.—General agitation. At the fireplace.)* I am just a little afraid of Patty. (PHŒBE *crosses to her and presses her hand. Enter* PATTY R., *a buxom young woman, who stands at the door.)* Patty, I hope we may not hurt your feelings, but— *(She loses courage.)*

PATTY *(advancing to* R.C.; *sternly).* Are you implicating, ma'am, that I have a follower?

SUSAN. Oh, no, Patty.

PATTY. So be it. *(She starts towards the door, retiring victorious.)*

*(*SUSAN *looks at* MISS WILLOUGHBY, *who is awfully ashamed.)*

SUSAN. Patty, come back. (PATTY *checks at the door and returns to* R.C.) I told you a falsehood just now. I am ashamed of myself.

PATTY. As well you might be, ma'am.

PHŒBE *(crossing to* C., *roused).* How dare you, woman! There *is* a man in the kitchen. I can see it in your face. To the door with him.

*(*MISS WILLOUGHBY, *above the settee, moves towards* SUSAN.)*

PATTY. A glorious soldier to be so treated!

PHŒBE. The door!

PATTY. And if he refuses?

*(*PHŒBE *turns to* MISS WILLOUGHBY *and* SUSAN. *They look blank.)*

SUSAN. Oh, dear!

PHŒBE *(to* PATTY). If he refuses—if he refuses—send him here—to me!

(She turns to MISS WILLOUGHBY *and* SUSAN, *who nod approval.* PATTY *glances at* MISS WILLOUGHBY, *then at* SUSAN, *curtsys, turns and exits* R.)*

SUSAN *(moving towards* PHŒBE). Lion-hearted Phœbe!

MISS WILLOUGHBY *(to L. of the settee)*. A soldier! *(Nervously.)* I wish it may not be that impertinent Recruiting Sergeant—I passed him in the street to-day. He closed one of his eyes at me—and then quickly opened it. *(Bridling.)* I knew what he meant.

SUSAN. What? Oh, that!

PHŒBE *(goes to the door R. and listens)*. He does not come. *(She comes down to R. settee.)*

SUSAN *(kneeling L.C.)*. I think I hear their voices in dispute. *(She puts her ear to the ground, listening.)*

(MISS WILLOUGHBY falls on her knees, L. of SUSAN, with her ear to the ground. PHŒBE also kneels. They all listen through the floor, and when they are in this position the RECRUITING SERGEANT enters R., unobserved. Standing in the doorway he gazes at them. They rise to their knees.)

MISS WILLOUGHBY. I distinctly hear him embracing her.

(ALL three listen on the ground again.)

SERGEANT. Do you, ma'am?

(They ALL start up. MISS WILLOUGHBY and SUSAN, with slight screams, exit down L. PHŒBE is following—but checks at L.C.)

PHŒBE *(turns)*. Sergeant!

SERGEANT *(comes down R.C., speaking with an Irish accent)*. Your sarvint, ma'am. *(He salutes.)*

(He drops his hand from the salute—PHŒBE retreats. She is as perplexed as he seems undismayed. She sees mud from his boots on the carpet.)

PHŒBE. Oh! Oh!—stop! *(She goes L., gets a paper*

from the work-table by the fireplace. She opens the paper once, looks at his boots and opens the paper fuller.) Sergeant, I am wishful to scold you but would you be so obliging as to stand on this paper while I do it? *(In a wheedling voice.)*

SERGEANT. With all the pleasure in life, ma'am.

PHŒBE *(spreading the paper on the floor).* Lift your feet— *(The* SERGEANT *lifts one foot.)* Both of them. *(The* SERGEANT *stands on the paper. She rises looking at him—eagerly.)* Sergeant, have you—killed people?

SERGEANT. Dozens, ma'am; dozens.

PHŒBE. How terrible! Oh, sir, I pray every night that the Lord in his loving kindness will root the enemy up. Is it true that the Corsican eats babies?

SERGEANT. I have seen him do it, ma'am.

PHŒBE. The man of sin! *(Half fearfully.)* Have you ever seen a vivandière, sir?

SERGEANT *(he gapes).* A what?

PHŒBE. A vivandière.

SERGEANT. Oh yes.

PHŒBE *(wistfully).* I have sometimes wished there were vivandières in the British Army. *(She marches a little L. She comes to herself and is shy, though he is admiring.)* Oh, Sergeant, a shudder goes through me when I see you in the streets enticing those poor young men.

SERGEANT. If you were one of them, ma'am, and death or glory was the call, *you* would take the shillings, ma'am.

PHŒBE. Oh, not for that.

SERGEANT *(springs to attention).* For *King* and *Country,* ma'am.

PHŒBE *(grandly).* Yes, yes, for that!

SERGEANT. Not that it's all fighting. The sack of captured towns. the loot—

PHŒBE *(proudly).* An English soldier never sacks or loots.

SERGEANT *(at attention).* No, ma'am! And then—the girls.

PHŒBE. What girls

SERGEANT. In the towns—that we don't sack.

PHŒBE *(proudly)*. How they must hate the haughty conqueror.

SERGEANT. We—we are not so haughty as all that. And—oh—of an evening you should see us marching down the street.

(Marching with an arm round an imaginary girl across to L.)

PHŒBE. But why do you hold your arm out?

SERGEANT. Why, ma'am— *(Again marching round.)* You see, 'tis a military custom, ma'am, that makes the Irish soldier loved all over the world.

PHŒBE. I think I understand. *(Sitting L.C., her eyes fall on the newspaper.)* Oh, Sergeant! *(The* SERGEANT *steps carefully over to* R.C. *and again stands on the paper.)* I fear, Sergeant, you do not tell those poor young men the noble things I thought you told them.

SERGEANT. Ma'am, I must e'en tell them what they are wishful to hear. There ha' been five men, all this week, listening to me, and then showing me their heels, but by a grand stroke of luck, I have them at last.

(SUSAN opens the door L., and listens.)

PHŒBE. Luck?

SERGEANT. The luck, ma'am, is that a gentleman of the town has enlisted. That gave them the push forward.

(SUSAN is excited.)

PHŒBE. A gentleman of this town enlisted. *(Rising eagerly.)* Sergeant, who?

SERGEANT. Why. ma'am. I think it be a secret as yet.

PHŒBE. But a gentleman! 'Tis the most amazing, exciting thing! *(Pressing.)* Sergeant, be so obliging!

SERGEANT. Nay, ma'am, I can't.

SUSAN (*comes on to* L., *carried away by excitement*). But you must! You must!

(*She checks, overcome with embarrassment, turns, and exits quickly* L. *The* SERGEANT *laughs. The door* L. *bangs—he looks at* PHŒBE, *who is confused.*)

PHŒBE. Sergeant, I have not been saying the things I meant to say to you. (*Coming to him a little.*) Will you please excuse my turning you out of the house somewhat violently?

SERGEANT. I am used to it, ma'am.

PHŒBE (*up to him at* C.). I won't really hurt you.

SERGEANT. Thank you kindly, ma'am.

(*The door* L. *squeaks*—PHŒBE *hears it, and assumes a stern expression.*)

PHŒBE (*in a loud voice, turning to face the door* L.—*The* SERGEANT *grins through this speech*). I protest, sir; we shall permit no followers in this house. Should I discover you in my kitchen again, I shall pitch you out—neck and crop. (*She turns to him.*) A glass of cowslip wine, sir? (*She goes up* L. *to the table.*)

SERGEANT. If not too strong, ma'am. (PHŒBE *pours out a glass of wine and brings it down to the* SERGEANT.) Thank you kindly, ma'am. (*He takes out a handkerchief and ties it round the stem of the glass.*)

(PHŒBE *is anxiously watching.*)

PHŒBE. Why do you do that, sir?

(*Another creak of the door.*)

SERGEANT. I was afraid I might swallow the glass. (*He drinks, holding the handkerchief with his left hand. He hands the glass to her.*)

PHŒBE *(friendly).* How strange! *(She takes the glass up to the table.* SUSAN *turns the handle of the door.* PHŒBE *comes down* L. *Very sternly.)* Begone, sir! *(The* SERGEANT *salutes. turns about and goes* R., PHŒBE *following him to* C.) Begone!

(The repetition, however lacks conviction. The SER-GEANT *turns at the door.* PHŒBE *curtsys. The* SER-GEANT *salutes, laughs and exits. All the ladies re-enter down* L., *admiring* PHŒBE, *who is conscious that this is undeserved. The visitors are in outdoor things.* SUSAN *leads the way, coming to* C. MISS WIL-LOUGHBY *comes to* L.C., *below the settee, with* FANNY *on her* L., *and slightly below.* HENRIETTA *is at down* L. PHŒBE *takes her muff from the settee and takes it up to the spinet.)*

MISS WILLOUGHBY (L. *of* SUSAN). Miss Phœbe, we could not but admire you.

*(*PHŒBE *falters.)*

SUSAN (C.). Phœbe of the lion heart!

*(*SUSAN *and* PHŒBE *go into the window opening.* MISS WILLOUGHBY *moves up* R. *of the settee* L.C. FANNY *at the* L. *end, and above it.* HENRIETTA, *to below the* L. *chair. The* SERGEANT *passes the window* R. *to* L. *He blows a kiss to* PHŒBE. ALL *start back, greatly shocked, as he passes on, disappearing* L.)*

PHŒBE *(moving down* R.). But the gentleman re-cruit—who can he be?

*(*FANNY *and* MISS WILLOUGHBY *move down* L., *near the stool.)*

MISS WILLOUGHBY *(moving to* C.). Yes, who?
SUSAN *(crossing from up* C., *to the bell rope above*

the fireplace), Perhaps they will know at the woollen drapers.

FANNY *(crossing to below the settee* L.C.). Let us inquire.

(SUSAN *moves down to below the chair* L.)

MISS WILLOUGHBY *(turning to* SUSAN). I wish to apologize. *(Crossing to* PHŒBE R.C., *sternly just.)* Miss Phœbe, you are a dear good girl. *(She curtsys—*PHŒBE *sits* R.C., *amazed.* MISS WILLOUGHBY *turns again to* SUSAN.) If I have made remarks about her ringlets, Susan—it was jealousy. *(She curtsys, crosses to the door* R., *which she opens.* FANNY *curtsys to* SUSAN, *turns and crosses to* PHŒBE.) Come, sister!

(PHŒBE *and* MISS SUSAN *are too startled to answer.* HENRIETTA *curtsys to* SUSAN *and follows across to* C.)

FANNY. Phœbe, dear, I wish you very happy.

PHŒBE *(rising).* Fanny!

(They embrace. FANNY *exits weeping, and is followed by* MISS WILLOUGHBY.)

HENRIETTA *(taking a pace towards* PHŒBE). Miss Phœbe, I give you joy.

(She curtsys shortly, and exits R., *weeping a little.* SUSAN, *a little bewildered, turns to the mantel.* PHŒBE *picks the paper from the floor and carries it to the hearth. During this, the door slams of* R., *and* HENRIETTA *is seen to pass the window, wiping her eyes. She is followed by a very small maid.)*

PHŒBE *(kneeling at the hearth).* Susan. You have been talking to them about V. B.

SUSAN (*sitting in the chair* L.). I could not help it. Now, Phœbe, what is it you have to tell me?

PHŒBE (*grown shy*). Dear, I think it is too holy to speak of. (*She rises, looking down at the fire.*)

SUSAN. To your sister?

PHŒBE (*almost in a whisper, sitting on the stool* L.). Well, as you know, I was sitting with an unhappy woman whose husband has fallen in the war. When I came out of the cottage he was passing. (*She is agitated.*)

SUSAN. Yes.

PHŒBE. He offered me his escort. At first he was very silent—as he has often been of late.

SUSAN. We know why.

PHŒBE. Please not to say that I know why. Suddenly he stopped and swung his cane. You know how gallantly he swings his cane.

SUSAN. Yes, indeed.

PHŒBE. It passed through me, sister, at that moment, how like he is to Julius Cæsar. He said, "I have something I am wishful to tell you, Miss Phœbe—perhaps you can guess what it is?"

SUSAN (*gasps*). Go on! Go on!

PHŒBE. To say I could guess, sister, would have been unladylike; I said: "Please not to tell me in the public thoroughfare," to which he instantly replied: "Then I shall call and tell you this afternoon."

SUSAN. Phœbe! (*She rises, coming to* R. *of* PHŒBE.)

PHŒBE (*rising*). Susan!

(*They embrace, but disengage as the door* R. *opens. PATTY enters with the tea-tray and goes across* L. *to the round table. PHŒBE carries the stool to below the* R. *end of the settee. SUSAN has moved up* C. *PATTY brings the small table and the tray to below the settee, and sets out the cups.*)

SUSAN. Did you meet with anyone while you were out, Phœbe?

PHŒBE. Did I or did I not? Yes, I bowed to Miss Barbara Meakin.

SUSAN. You did not enter into conversation!

PHŒBE. Not absolutely—I said "How do you do"—but—without stopping or waiting for the reply.

SUSAN *(above the settee)*. That was sufficient. Why, Patty, you have brought three cups.

PATTY *(R. of the table)*. I thought, ma'am, that one of you might be having a follower.

(She crosses, with a secret smile of triumph, and exits R. Then the sisters exchange glances and simper. SUSAN takes a chair to L. of the table, and sits.)

PHŒBE *(crossing slowly to the stool R. of the table)*. Susan, to think that it has all happened in a single year. *(She stands, in thought.)*

(SUSAN puts milk and sugar in the cups. They keep exchanging delighted little glances throughout this scene, at the tea-table; but there is not much audible laughter.)

SUSAN *(during business)*. Such a genteel competency as he can offer—such a desirable establishment.

PHŒBE. I had not thought of that, dear. *(She sits on the stool.)* I was recalling our first meeting at Mrs. Fotheringay's quadrille party.

SUSAN. We were not even aware that our respected local physician had a new partner. *(She gives PHŒBE tea.)*

PHŒBE. Until he said "Allow me to present my new partner, Mr. Valentine Brown." *(She raises her cup as if to toast him.)*

SUSAN *(sniggering)*. Phœbe, do you remember how at the tea-table he facetiously passed the cake basket with nothing in it?

PHŒBE *(with a twitter of merriment)*. He was so

amusing from the first. *(Earnestly.)* I am thankful, Susan, that I, too, have a sense of humour. I am exceedingly funny at times, am I not, Susan?

SUSAN. Yes. indeed! But he sees humour in the most unexpected things. I say something so ordinary about loving, for instance, to have everything in this room either blue or white and I know not why he laughs, but it makes me feel quite witty.

(They laugh.)

PHŒBE *(a little anxiously)*. I hope he sees nothing odd or quaint about us.

SUSAN. My dear, whatever we are, we are not that.

(PATTY enters R. with two plates with cake and biscuits. They are immediately primly engaged at tea without looking at her.)

PHŒBE. Did I tell you, Susan, that I met Miss Barbara Meakin while I was out?

SUSAN. Did you, or did you not?

PHŒBE. She was purchasing a Whimsey cake.

SUSAN. Another! That makes the second this week.

(Exit PATTY R., smirking.)

PHŒBE. Susan, the picnics. *(She takes a cake.)*

SUSAN. Phœbe, the day when he first drank tea in this house!

PHŒBE. He invited himself.

SUSAN. He merely laughed when I said it would cause such talk.

PHŒBE. He is absolutely fearless! Susan, he has smoked his pipe in this room.

(They are both a little scared.)

SUSAN. Smoking is indeed a dreadful habit!

PHŒBE. But there is something so dashing about it.

SUSAN (*a pause—with melancholy, putting the cup on the saucer*). And now I am to be left alone.

PHŒBE (*puts down her cup and saucer*). No! (*She looks at* SUSAN *a little tensely.*)

SUSAN. Oh yes, my dear, I could not leave this room. My lovely blue and white room. (*She looks around at it, with affection.*)

PHŒBE (*who has become agitated*). Susan, you must make my house your home. I—I have something very distressing to tell you.

SUSAN (*startled*). My dear!

(PHŒBE *turns, on the stool, to face down stage.*)

PHŒBE. You know Mr. Brown advised us how to invest half of our money?

SUSAN (*stirring her tea*). I know it gives us eight per cent, though why it should do so I cannot understand, but very obliging I am sure. (*She drinks her tea.*)

PHŒBE. Susan, (*a slight hesitation*) —all the money is lost. (SUSAN *lowers her cup, staring.*) I had the letter several days ago. (*She is not looking at* SUSAN.)

SUSAN. Lost! (*She puts down her cup and saucer on the table.*)

PHŒBE. Something burst, dear, and then—they absconded.

SUSAN. But Mr. Brown—

PHŒBE (*turning and leaning earnestly towards* SUSAN). I have not apprised him of it yet—for he will think it was his fault—but I shall tell him to-day.

SUSAN. Phœbe, how much have we left?

PHŒBE. Only sixty pounds a year, so you see you must live with us, dearest.

SUSAN. But Mr. Brown, he—

PHŒBE (*grandly, facing down* L.). Mr. Brown is a man of means, and if he is not proud to have my Susan, I shall say at once: "Mr. Brown, the door."

SUSAN *(softly)*. Phœbe, I have a wedding gift for you.

PHŒBE. Not yet.

SUSAN. It has been ready for a long time. *(A slight pause.)* I began it— *(She breaks off. Then, calling.)* Patty!

PHŒBE *(puzzled)*. Patty!

(SUSAN rises, goes L. and rings the bell, comes back and takes her chair to L.)

SUSAN. One cannot be too careful.

PHŒBE *(enlightened)*. No, indeed. *(She rises and goes up C., to the windows, staring out.)*

(Enter PATTY R. She stands in the doorway, waiting.)

SUSAN. Thank you, Patty. (PATTY *crosses, takes the table and tray to L., above the fireplace.)* When you met Miss Barbara Meakin, Phœbe, was she accompanied by her little dog? *(Putting on the glove and removing the kettle from the fire to the hob.)*

PHŒBE *(turning, at up C.)*. Was she, or was she not? I certainly cannot remember seeing the dog.

(PATTY takes up the tray and crosses R.)

SUSAN. She may have left it at home.

PHŒBE *(moving a little L.C., above the settee)*. True, and that would account for its absence.

(PATTY tries to close the door with her foot.)

SUSAN *(seeing PATTY's business and crossing C.)*. Patty, how often have I told you not to shut the door with your foot? *(She turns to pick up the stool.)*

(PATTY checks, looks at SUSAN, sees she is not looking and exits, closing the door with her foot. SUSAN

takes the stool down L.. *and returns to below the* R.
end of the settee and sits.)

PHŒBE *(to* L. *of the settee)*. Susan, this wedding
gift. *(She sits* L. *of* SUSAN.)

SUSAN. I began it when I was a young woman and
you were not ten years old. I meant it for myself,
Phœbe, I had hoped that he—his name was William,
but I think I must have been too unattractive, my love.

PHŒBE. Sweetest—dearest—

SUSAN. I always associate it with a sprigged poplin
I was wearing that summer, with a breadth of coloured
silk in it, being a naval officer; but something happened
—a Miss Cicely Pemberton—and they are quite big
boys now. So long ago, Phœbe—he was very tall with
brown eyes—it was most foolish of me, but I was always so fond of sewing—with long straight legs and
such a pleasant expression.

(A pause. PHŒBE *is gazing at* SUSAN, *who, with a little
smile and a tiny sigh, looks down at her hands.)*

PHŒBE. Susan, what was it?

SUSAN *(looking up at* PHŒBE, *quite brightly)*. It
was a wedding-gown, my dear—even plain women,
Phœbe, we cannot help it, when we are young, we have
romantic ideas, just as if we were pretty.

PHŒBE. Susan, you are very pretty! Your eyes—

SUSAN. I have sometimes thought that my eyes were
not wholly disagreeable.

PHŒBE. Your profile.

SUSAN. Perhaps the right side of my face has a certain charm, but the left! He always sat on my left side,
Phœbe, and so—the wedding gown was never used.

PHŒBE. Darling!

SUSAN. Long before it was finished, I knew he would
not offer, but I finished it and put it away. *(She rises
and crosses to* R.) I have always hidden it from you,

Phœbe, but of late I have brought it out again *(unlocking a drawer in the bureau)* and altered it.

PHŒBE *(rising, comes down* L.C.*).* Susan, I could not wear it. (SUSAN *takes out the gown and holds it up. Crossing to* R.C.*)* Oh, how sweet—how beautiful! *(She takes the dress and moves* L.C., *and sits, smoothing and admiring it.)*

SUSAN *(moving up to above* R. *end of the settee* L.C.*).* You will wear it, my love, won't you? (PHŒBE *nods, looking down at the dress.)* And the tears it was sewn with long ago will all turn into smiles on my Phœbe's wedding day.

(She bends over PHŒBE, *who puts her face up. They kiss.)*

PHŒBE. Tears. *(She kisses the dress.)* Tears—tears. *(A knock at the street door is heard. Rising.)* That knock! *(She faces* R., *holding out the dress.)*

SUSAN. Always so dashing. *(She takes the gown from* PHŒBE.*)*

PHŒBE *(turning and moving down* L.C.*).* Always so imperious! *(Turning to* SUSAN, *suddenly panic-stricken.)* Susan! I think he kissed me once!

*(*SUSAN *smiles, then, startled, puts the gown on the settee* R.C. *and moves to up* C.*)*

SUSAN. You *think?*

PHŒBE *(moving away).* I *know* he did. *(She checks, as she remembers.)* That evening—a week ago when he was squiring me home from the concert. It was raining and my face was wet— *(with a quick side glance—as if this were an extenuating circumstance)* he said that was why he did it.

SUSAN. Because your face was wet?

PHŒBE *(ruefully, as she crosses slowly* R.C.*).* It does not seem a sufficient excuse now.

SUSAN (*appalled. coming down* L.C.). Oh, Phœbe, before he had offered.

PHŒBE (*turning up* R.C., *in distress*). I fear me it was most unladylike.

SUSAN. Ssh!

(PHŒBE *goes to the spinet.* SUSAN *sits in the armchair* L., *taking work from the settee. Enter* PATTY R., *going below the door.*)

PATTY. Mr. Brown!

(SUSAN *rises, coming down* L.C. *Enter* VALENTINE *down* R. *He is a frank, genial young man of twenty-five, who honestly admires the ladies, though he is amused by their quaintness. He gives his hat, stick and gloves to* PATTY.)

VALENTINE. Thank you, Patty. (*Crossing down to* SUSAN.) Miss Susan, how do you do, ma'am?

(*They shake hands as* PATTY *exits and* PHŒBE *comes down* R.C.)

SUSAN. This is indeed a surprise, I had no idea it was you.

VALENTINE (*turning* R. *to* PHŒBE). Nay, Miss Phœbe, though we have met to-day already I insist on shaking hands with you again.

(*They shake hands.*)

SUSAN. Always so dashing!

(VALENTINE *laughs heartily, crosses up* R.C., *taking off his coat. The ladies resume their seats and exchange delighted smiles,* PHŒBE R.C., SUSAN L.C.)

VALENTINE (*putting his coat on the music-stool*). And

my other friends, I hope I find them in health. *(To* SUSAN.*)* The spinet, ma'am, seems quite herself to-day; I trust the ottoman passed a good night.

SUSAN *(pleased)*. Indeed, sir, we are all quite well.

VALENTINE *(coming down L. of the R.C. settee)*. May I sit on this couch, Miss Phœbe? I know Miss Susan likes me to break her couches.

SUSAN. Indeed, sir, I do not. Phœbe, how strange that he should think so.

PHŒBE *(a little wistfully)*. The remark was humorous, was it not?

VALENTINE. How you see through me, Miss Phœbe. *(He punches a cushion and proceeds to roll up a coverlet.)*

(The sisters again exchange delighted smiles.)

SUSAN *(thinking aloud)*. Oh dear, I feel sure **he is** to roll the coverlet into a ball and then sit **on it!**

(Looks between VALENTINE *and* PHŒBE.*)*

PHŒBE *(sotto voce)*. Mr. Brown!

*(*VALENTINE *checks himself and abstains. He sits, laughing, L. of* PHŒBE.*)*

VALENTINE *(turning from one to the other)*. So I am dashing, Miss Susan! Am I dashing, Miss Phœbe? PHŒBE. A little. I think.

*(*VALENTINE *and the ladies laugh.)*

VALENTINE. Well, I have something to tell you to-day, which I really think *is* rather dashing.

*(*SUSAN *rises and is going* L.*)*

SUSAN. One moment—

(VALENTINE *rises and moves to* C. PHŒBE *rises, turns*
      R., *and up to the spinet.*)

VALENTINE (*to* SUSAN). You are not going, ma'am,
before you know what it is?
      SUSAN (*turning at the door* L.). I—I—indeed—to be
sure—I—I—know, Mr. Brown.
      PHŒBE (*at the spinet, facing down* L.). Susan!
      SUSAN. I mean I do not know, Mr. Brown—I mean
I can guess—I mean, Phœbe, my love, explain.

(*She exits* L., *taking her work with her.* VALENTINE
      pulls a face, moves a little L., *and then turns to face
      up to* PHŒBE.)

VALENTINE. The explanation being, I suppose, that
you both know—and I had flattered myself 'twas such
a secret! Am I then to understand that you had fore-
seen it all, Miss Phœbe?
      PHŒBE (*seated at the spinet, alarmed*). Nay, sir,
you must not ask that.
      VALENTINE (*turning up to the fire*). I believe in any
case, 'twas you who first put it into my head. (*He
warms his hands.*)
      PHŒBE (*aghast*). Oh, I hope not.

(*During this* PHŒBE *is half turned away from him
      towards the spinet.*)

VALENTINE (*reminiscently, looking out front*).
Your demure eyes flashed so every time the war was
mentioned—the little Quaker suddenly looked like a
gallant boy in ringlets.

(*A terrible fear comes over* PHŒBE. *She turns her
      head slowly to look at* VALENTINE. *A slight pause.
      Then:*)

PHŒBE (*rising*). Mr. Brown, what is it you have to
tell us?

VALENTINE *(turning, with his back to the fire)*. That I have enlisted, Miss Phœbe. Why? Did you surmise it was something else

PHŒBE *(coming down a pace or two to* C.*)*. You are going to the war?

VALENTINE. Yes.

PHŒBE. Mr. Brown, is it a jest?

VALENTINE. It would be a sorry jest, ma'am, but I—I thought from what Miss Susan said that you knew. I concluded the recruiting sergeant had talked.

PHŒBE. The recruiting sergeant—I see. *(She turns down* R.C. *and sits at the* L. *end of the settee.)*

VALENTINE *(as he moves* C.*)*. These stirring times, Miss Phœbe, he is but half a man who stays at home. I have chafed for months. I want to see if I have any courage. And as to be an army surgeon does not appeal to me, it was enlist or remain behind. *(Turning at up* C.*, to face down* R.*)* To-day, I found that there were five waverers—I asked them, would they take the shilling if I took it, and they assented. *(Coming down a pace or two.)* Miss Phœbe, it is not one man I give to the King, but six.

PHŒBE *(looking at her hands)*. I think you have done bravely.

VALENTINE. We leave shortly for Petersburgh barracks, and I go to London to-morrow—so this is goodbye.

PHŒBE *(gazing out front)*. I shall pray that you may be preserved in battle, Mr. Brown.

VALENTINE *(going to above the* R. *end of the settee* R.C.*)*. And you and Miss Susan will write to me when occasion offers?

PHŒBE. If you wish it.

VALENTINE. With all the stirring news of Quality Street?

PHŒBE. It has seemed stirring to us—it must have been merely laughable to you who came from a great city.

VALENTINE *(laughs)*. Dear Quality Street—that

thought me dashing. *(He sits* R. *of* PHŒBE.) But I made friends in it, Miss Phœbe—of two very sweet ladies.

PHŒBE. Mr. Brown, I wonder why you have been so kind to my sister and me?

VALENTINE. Nay—the kindness was yours. If at first Miss Susan amused me— *(chuckling—indicating bows)* to see her on her knees decorating the little legs of the couch with frills as if it were a child. *(Sincerely.)* But it was her sterling qualities that impressed me presently.

PHŒBE *(bravely—looking at him)*. And did—did I amuse you also?

VALENTINE. Prodigiously, Miss Phœbe. (PHŒBE *laughs a little hysterically.)* Those other ladies—they were always scolding you—your youthfulness shocked them. I believe they thought you dashing.

PHŒBE. I have sometimes feared that I was perhaps *too* dashing.

(VALENTINE *roars at this.*)

VALENTINE. You delicious Miss Phœbe! You were too quiet! I felt sorry that one so sweet and young should live so grey a life. I wondered whether I could put any little pleasure into it.

PHŒBE. The picnics! Oh, it was very good of you!

VALENTINE. That was only how it began, for soon I knew that it was I who got the pleasures and you who gave them. You have been to me, Miss Phœbe, like a quiet old-fashioned garden full of flowers that English-men love best, because they have known them longest, the daisy that stands for innocence, and the hyacinth for constancy, and the modest violet. and the rose. When I am far away, ma'am, I shall often think of Miss Phœbe's pretty soul, which is her garden, and shut my eyes and walk in it.

(PHŒBE *turns to hide her pain. Enter* SUSAN, *in a twitter,* L.)

SUSAN (*coming a little towards* L.C.). Have you—
is it— (VALENTINE *rises.* PHŒBE *runs across to her*
L. VALENTINE *moves up* R.C.) You seem so calm,
Phœbe.

PHŒBE (*pressing her hand warningly and imploringly*). Susan, what Mr. Brown is so obliging as to inform us of is not what we expected—not that at all.
My dear, *he* is the gentleman who has enlisted, and he
came to tell us that and to say good-bye.

VALENTINE (*coming down* C.). Yes, that is it.

SUSAN. Going away?

PHŒBE. Yes, dear!

VALENTINE. Am I not the ideal recruit, ma'am, a
man without a wife, or a mother, or a sweetheart?

SUSAN. No sweetheart?

VALENTINE. Have you one for me, Miss Susan?

(PHŒBE *is in terror lest* SUSAN *will divulge the
situation.*)

PHŒBE (*at* L.C., *briskly*). Susan, we shall have to tell
him now. You dreadful man, you will laugh and say
it is just like Quality Street, but indeed since I met you
to-day and you told me you had something to com-
municate we have been puzzling what it could be—
and we concluded that you were to be married!

VALENTINE. Ha! ha! ha! Was that it?

PHŒBE. So like women, you know, we thought we
perhaps knew her. We were even discussing what we
should wear at the wedding.

VALENTINE. Ha, ha! I shall often think of this. I
wonder who would have me, Miss Susan? But I must
be off— (*He goes to the music-stool for his coat*) —and
God bless you both.

(PHŒBE *moves up* C., *to* R. *of the settee.*)

SUSAN. You are going?

VALENTINE (*coming down to* SUSAN, *taking both*

her hands). No more mud on your carpet, Miss Susan, no more coverlets rolled into balls. A good riddance. *(He kisses* SUSAN'S *hands as* PHŒBE *moves across to the spinet. Turning up to* PHŒBE.) Miss Phœbe, a last look at the garden. *(He takes both her hands.)*

PHŒBE (R. *of* VALENTINE). We shall miss you very much, Mr. Brown.

(VALENTINE *kisses her hand, and crosses her to the door* R. *The snow falls again.)*

VALENTINE *(checking at the door, remembering).* There is one little matter—that investment I advised you to make—I am happy it has turned out so well.
SUSAN *(taking a pace* C., *about to tell).* Mr. Brown—

(PHŒBE *goes down to her and checks her.)*

PHŒBE *(turning to look at* VALENTINE). It was good of you to take all that trouble, sir. Accept our grateful thanks.

(They stand down L.C. PHŒBE *to* R. *of and slightly above* SUSAN.)

VALENTINE. Nay, I am glad that you are so comfortably left. *(He goes down to them and puts his hands on their shoulders.)* I am your big brother. Good-bye again. *(He goes to the door* R., *and turns.)* This little blue and white room and its dear inmates—may they be unchanged if I—when I come back. Good-bye.

(He bows. PHŒBE *and* SUSAN *curtsy. Exit* VALENTINE R., *closing the door.* PHŒBE *takes one pace towards it and stops. The hall door slams. A slight pause.* MISS SUSAN *looks apprehensively at* PHŒBE. PHŒBE, *trying hard to be calm, smiles pitifully, turning to* SUSAN.)

PHŒBE. Smile, Susan. *(She turns her face away and then moves up a little, towards the window.* VALENTINE *passes outside,* R. *to* L. PHŒBE *curtsys and he raises his hat.* SUSAN *sits at the* L. *end of the settee* L.C.) A misunderstanding—just a mistake! (SUSAN *sobs.* PHŒBE *turns down to her.*) Don't, dear, don't! *(She remains calm by an effort.)* We can live it down. *(She crosses* R., *puts the dress in the bureau, locks the drawer, and returning* L.C., *gives the key to* SUSAN.)

SUSAN. He is a fiend in human form.

PHŒBE. Nay, you hurt me, sister. *(She turns a pace* R.) He is a brave gentleman.

SUSAN. The money—why did you not let me tell him?

PHŒBE *(facing* SUSAN). So that he might offer to me out of pity? Susan!   *(WARN Curtain.)*

SUSAN. Phœbe, how are we to live—with the quarter loaf at one and tenpence.

PHŒBE. Brother James—

SUSAN. You know very well that Brother James will do nothing for us.

PHŒBE *(going to her)*. I think, Susan, we could keep a little school—for genteel children only, of course. *(She sits* R. *of* SUSAN.) I would do most of the teaching.

SUSAN. You a schoolmistress—Phœbe of the ringlets! Everyone would laugh.

PHŒBE. I shall hide the ringlets in a cap like yours, Susan, and people will soon forget them. And I shall try to look staid and to grow old quickly. It will not be so hard to me as you think, dear.

SUSAN. There were other gentlemen—they were attracted by you, Phœbe—and you turned from them.

PHŒBE *(quietly, smiling)*. I did not want them.

SUSAN *(her hand on* PHŒBE's *lap)*. They will come again—and others.

PHŒBE *(putting her hand over* SUSAN's). No, dear, never speak of that to me, any more. *(Remembering.)* I let him kiss me—

SUSAN (earnestly). You could not prevent him!

PHŒBE. Yes, I could, I know I could now. (Withdrawing her hand slowly.) I wanted him to do it. Oh, never speak to me of others after that. Perhaps he saw I wanted it, and did it to please me! But I meant, indeed I did—that I gave it to him with all my love; he did not love me and I let him kiss me. (Her hands go to her cheeks.) Oh, sister, I could bear all the rest—but—I have been unladylike.

(They turn from each other, heads hanging.)

CURTAIN.

ACT TWO

SCENE.—*The same room, but it has been turned into a schoolroom.*

Most of the old furniture is gone, but some of it remains, including the spinet, settee, cabinet, and one chair, to suggest that the apartment is still used as a living-room. There is a high teacher's desk R. Two forms near each other are L.C., up stage. On the walls are some large old-fashioned wall maps. The centre of this room is devoid of furniture and there is a white cloth on the floor to save the carpet. A large globe stands down stage R. and a smaller one is on the spinet. There is a small form L. of the desk R. (See Ground Plan.)

The CURTAIN *rises on* PHŒBE *teaching a dancing lesson to four little boys and four little girls, who are in the quaint costume of the period. Ten years have elapsed since the last act, but* PHŒBE *looks twenty years older. Her curls are out of sight under her cap, her dress and manners are very prim. She is very patient and sweet with the pupils, but lifeless, as if she had lost all her sparkle. The more set her figure looks the better it will be for what is to follow. From the way in which she occasionally presses her hand to her forehead it is evident that she has a headache. On the settee up* C. *stands a little boy (*ARTHUR*) with a dunce's cap on his head. Children up and down* L. *of* C. *Girls* R., *boys* L.

The time is August—ten years later.

As the CURTAIN *rises,* PHŒBE *plays a chord and the first part of the dance through. The children dance.*

35

PHŒBE (during the music). Now, toes out! Keep in line. (Turning her head as she plays.) Chest, Georgie! (GEORGIE throws out his stomach. At the end of the first part, PHŒBE comes down R.C.) Miss Beveridge, point your toes so. (She dances, singing the air.) Now keep in line and, young ladies, do think of your toes. (Going up to the spinet, she sits.) Now! (She plays the second part as they dance. At the end of the dance, she comes down R.C.) That will do. You may sit down. (They go up L.C., and sit on the forms, whispering. Bus. To GEORGIE, who is behind the rest.) You remain where you are. (GEORGIE has been valiantly shoving out a part of his person lower than his chest and now does it more than ever out of a noble desire to give satisfaction. PHŒBE surveys him sadly.) Oh, Georgie, do you not know which is your chest? (GEORGIE sticks out his stomach. PHŒBE turns and gets the chalk from the desk. She kneels R. of him. He sticks his stomach out further. She draws a "C" on his jacket.) "C" stands for chest, Georgie. (She looks at the protruding part and taps it.) This is "S."

(SUSAN darts out of the room L., coming to C.,—L. of GEORGIE.)

SUSAN (putting her hands over GEORGIE's ears, turning his head to L. and speaking in a quick, low voice). Phœbe, how many are fourteen and seventeen?

PHŒBE. Thirty-one.

SUSAN. I thank you.

(She turns GEORGIE's head to the front again and darts off L.)

PHŒBE. That will do, ladies and gentlemen. You may go. (The children, except ARTHUR, rise, bow and curtsy, go to the door and exit L. GEORGE is last but one.) Chest, Georgie! (GEORGIE protrudes his stomach and exits. The last child, ISABELLA, remains behind. She is a for-

bidding-looking, learned little girl. ISABELLA *rises and holds up her hand for permission to speak.*) What is it, Isabella?

ISABELLA *(coming to* L. *of* PHŒBE). Please, ma'am, Father wishes me to acquire algebra.

PHŒBE *(alarmed).* Algebra! It—it is not a very ladylike study, Isabella.

ISABELLA. Father says will you, or won't you?

PHŒBE. And you're thin—it will make you thinner, my dear.

ISABELLA. Father says I'm thin, but wiry.

PHŒBE. Yes, you are. You are very wiry, Isabella.

ISABELLA. Father says either I acquire algebra, or I go to Miss Prother's establishment.

PHŒBE *(faintly).* Very well, I—I shall do my best. You may go. *(She sits wearily on the form* R.)

(Exits ISABELLA L.—*after a curtsy—with her nose in the air.)*

ARTHUR *(who ·s standing on the settee).* Please, ma'am, may I take it off now

PHŒBE. Certainly not! *(With presence of mind.)* Unhappy boy! (ARTHUR *grins.*) Come here! (ARTHUR *descends and comes down* R.C. *She takes off his cap.*) Are you ashamed of yourself?

ARTHUR. No, ma'am. *(Brightly.)*

PHŒBE *(in a terrible voice).* Arthur Wellesley Thomson, fetch me the implement. *(She puts the cap under the desk.* ARTHUR *blithely brings the cane from the table up* L. *and gives it to* PHŒBE. *She hits the form with it, three times.)* Arthur, surely that terrifies you?

ARTHUR. No, ma'am.

PHŒBE. Arthur, why did you fight that street boy?

ARTHUR. 'Cos he said when you caned you didn't draw blood.

PHŒBE. But I don't, do I?

ARTHUR. No, ma'am.

PHŒBE. Then why fight him? Was it more for the honour of the school?

ARTHUR. Yes, ma'am.

PHŒBE. Say you are sorry, Arthur, and I won't punish you.

(ARTHUR *bursts into tears.*)

ARTHUR (*blubbering, his knuckles in his eyes*). You promised to cane me and now you aren't going to do it.

PHŒBE (*incredulously—rising*). Do you *wish* to be caned?

ARTHUR (*eagerly holds his hand out*). If you please, Miss Phœbe.

PHŒBE. Unnatural boy! (*She canes him in a very unprofessional manner.*) Poor dear boy! (*She kisses the hand.*)

ARTHUR (*gloomily*). Oh, ma'am, you will never be able to cane if you hold it like that. (*Illustrating.*) You should hold it like this, and give it a wriggle like that. Pht! ! (*Imitating the swish of the cane.*)

PHŒBE (*imitates the movement*). Pht! (*Almost in tears.*) Go away! (*She sits on the form* L. *of the desk.*)

ARTHUR (*going towards her, he sits on her knee*). Don't cry, ma'am. I love you, Miss Phœbe. And if any boy says you can't cane, I'll blood him, Miss Phœbe.

(PHŒBE *shudders—*SUSAN *darts in* L. ARTHUR *stands.*)

PHŒBE (*As* SUSAN *signs that* ARTHUR *is in the way*). Run away, run away!

(*She gives* ARTHUR *a gentle push, and a smile which he returns, before running across* L., *and off.*)

SUSAN (*as soon as* ARTHUR *is gone*). Phœbe, if a herring and a half cost three ha'pence. how many for elevenpence?

PHŒBE *(instantly)*. Eleven.

SUSAN. William Smith says it is fifteen, and he is such a big boy. Do you think I ought to contradict him? May I say there are differences of opinion about it? No one can be *really* sure, Phœbe.

PHŒBE. It is eleven. I once worked it out with real herrings. *(She rises and goes to her,* C.) Susan, we must never let the big boys think that we are afraid of them. To awe them, stamp with the foot, speak in a ferocious voice, and look them unflinchingly in the face. *(She stamps her foot.* SUSAN *imitates her. The band is heard playing softly, in the distance.)* Oh, Susan. Isabella's father insists on her acquiring algebra!

SUSAN *(groans)*. What is algebra exactly? Is it those three-cornered little things?

PHŒBE. It is X minus Y equals Z plus Y—and things like that. And all the time you are saying they are equal, you feel in your heart, "Why should they be?" *(The band is loud.* A YOKEL *goes across* L. *to* R. PHŒBE *turns down behind the desk and sits there.* SUSAN *moves up* C., *to the window.)* It is the band for to-night's ball. It is not every year that there is a Waterloo to celebrate.

SUSAN. I was not thinking of that. *(Turning to look at* PHŒBE.) I was thinking that he is to be at the ball to-night, and we have not seen him for ten years.

PHŒBE *(calmly, selecting a book)*. Yes, ten years. We shall be glad to welcome our old friend back, Susan. *(She opens a Latin book.)* I am going into your room now to take the Latin class.

SUSAN. Oh, that weary Latin! *(Moving down* L.) I wish I had the whipping of the man who invented it.

(She sighs and exits L. PHŒBE *goes over a declension aloud. The band stops.)*

PHŒBE *(seated at the desk)*. Labor, labour, laboris, of labour, labori, to labour, laborem, labour, labor oh labour. *(With feeling.)* Oh. labour! *(Her head on the*

desk. Re-enter MISS SUSAN *excitedly,* L. *Looking up.)*
What is it?

SUSAN *(tragically, as she comes to* C.). Phœbe—
William Smith! I tried to look ferocious, indeed I did.
but he saw I was afraid and before the whole school he
put out his tongue at me. *(She hides her face.)*

PHŒBE. Susan! *(She rises, gets the cane from the
desk and comes to* C.)

SUSAN *(as if to intercept her)*. Phœbe, he is much too
big. Let it pass.

PHŒBE (C.). If I let it pass I am a stumbling-block
in the way of true education.

SUSAN *(getting in her way imploringly)*. Sister!

PHŒBE *(grandly)*. Susan, stand aside. *(She waves
her away, crosses to near the door* L.—*remembers*
ARTHUR'S *instructions—flicks the cane.)* Pht!!

*(Nodding to assure herself that is the proper way, she
marches off* L.. *the cane on her shoulder.* SUSAN
closes the door L. *and is listening in apprehension.*
PATTY *ushers in* CAPTAIN VALENTINE BROWN, R.
*He looks his ten years older, and is bronzed and
soldierly. He wears the whiskers of the period and is
in uniform. He has lost his left hand, but this is not
at first noticeable. He comes towards* SUSAN.)

PATTY. Miss Susan, 'tis Captain Brown.

SUSAN *(turning with a start)*. Captain Brown! *(She
moves to meet him up* C.)

VALENTINE. Reports himself at home again. *(He
clicks his heels and shakes hands warmly.)* Miss Susan!

SUSAN *(gratified)*. You call this home?

(Exit PATTY R., *leaving the door open.)*

VALENTINE. When the other men talked of their
homes, Miss Susan, I thought of—this room. *(He goes
down* R., *turns back to up* C., *then faces* L., *looking about
him.)* Maps—desks—heigho! But still it is the same

dear room. *(He crosses* L., *and turns.)* I have often dreamt, Miss Susan, that I came back to it in muddy shoes. *(Seeing her alarm.)* I have not, you know. *(Up to her, touching her shoulder.)* Miss Susan, I rejoice to find no change in you, and Miss Phœbe—Miss Phœbe of the ringlets—I hope there be as little change in her?

SUSAN *(painfully)*. Phœbe of the ringlets. Ah, sir, you need not expect to see her. *(She turns up to the settee.)*

VALENTINE *(very disappointed)*. She is not here. I vow it spoils all my homecoming.

(The door L. *is flung open and* PHŒBE *rushes out, followed by* WILLIAM SMITH *who is brandishing the cane. At* L.C., VALENTINE *takes in the situation and, without looking at* PHŒBE, *takes* WILLIAM *by the collar and marches him off* R. PHŒBE *collapses on the form* L. *of the desk.)*

SUSAN *(coming down* R.C.*)*. Phœbe, did you see who it is?

PHŒBE. I saw! *(In sudden panic.)* Susan, I have lost all my looks.

(Enter the children L., *crowding in the doorway.* SUSAN *crosses* L., *pushing them back to the other room.)*

SUSAN. Children, go back. To your places—begin your multiplication tables *(etc., ad lib. She urges them off and exits with them, closing the door. Re-enter* VALENTINE R.*)*

VALENTINE *(speaking as he enters and not realizing it is* PHŒBE *as her back is to him)*. A young reprobate, ma'am. *(He closes the door and comes* C.*)* But I have deposited him in the causeway. *(He sees* PHŒBE.*)* I fear— *(He stops, puzzled, because she has covered her face with her hands.)*

PHŒBE. Captain Brown!

VALENTINE *(startled)*. Miss Phœbe—it is you?

(He goes to her and she drops her hands. He understands her distress but cannot help showing that her appearance is a shock to him.)

PHŒBE *(bitterly)*. Yes, I have changed very much. I have not worn well, Captain Brown!

VALENTINE *(awkwardly)*. We—we—are both older, Miss Phœbe. *(He holds out a hand kindly with affected high spirits.)*

PHŒBE. It was both hands when you went away! *(VALENTINE has to show her that the left hand is gone. She is pained. Rising, with a cry.)* I did not know. You never mentioned it in your letters.

VALENTINE. Miss Phœbe, what did you omit from your letters—that you had such young blackguards as that to terrify you.

PHŒBE. He is the only one—most of them are little dears—and this is the last day of the term.

VALENTINE *(turning up* L.C.*)*. Ah, ma'am, if only you had invested all your money as you laid out part by my advice. *(He faces her.)* What a monstrous pity you did not.

PHŒBE. We—never thought of it.

VALENTINE. You look so tired.

PHŒBE *(smiles up at him wearily)*. I have the headache to-day.

VALENTINE. You did not use to have the headache. Curse those little dears! *(He stamps and sits on the form* L.*)*

PHŒBE *(to* L.C.*)*. Nay, do not distress yourself about me. *(She sits on the form* L.C.*)* Tell me of yourself. We are so proud of the way in which you won your commission—shall you leave the Army now?

VALENTINE. Yes, and I have some intention of pursuing again the old life in Quality Street. *(He is very depressed.)* I came here in such high spirits. Miss

Phœbe— *(He rises, stands on her left, one foot on the form, elbow on knee.)*

PHŒBE *(bitterly).* The change in me depresses you!

VALENTINE. I was in hopes that you and Miss Susan would be going to the ball. I had brought cards for you with me to make sure.

(PHŒBE is pleased and means to accept. He sighs and she understands he thinks her too old.)

PHŒBE. Yes! But now you see that my dancing days are done.

VALENINE. Ah, no!

(He sighs, straightening up. She is bitter, but calm.)

PHŒBE *(pleasantly).* But you will find many charming partners at the ball. Many of them have been pupils of mine. There was even a pupil of mine who fought at Waterloo.

VALENTINE *(crossing her to c.).* Young Blades— I—I have heard him on it. *(PHŒBE puts her hand to her head. Passionately, turning to face her.)* Miss Phœbe, what a dull grey world it is. *(He turns up c.)*

(PHŒBE turns away to hide her emotion. Re-enter SUSAN L., leaving the door open. She crosses and opens the R. door.)

SUSAN *(as she crosses).* Phœbe, I have said that you will not take the Latin class to-day, and am dismissing them.

VALENTINE. Latin! *(He crosses down, L. of the desk.)*

PHŒBE *(rising—defiantly).* I am proud to teach it. Susan, his hand—have you seen? *(Pointing to VALENTINE'S sleeve.)*

SUSAN *(moving in to R.C.).* Oh, oh! *(Appealingly. The children come in L.. about fifteen of them. They*

*are now in caps, etc.—some of the boys are half martial
in appearance as they wear caps in imitation of the
Army.)* Hats off—gentlemen salute, ladies curtsy—
(The children obey.) —to the gallant Captain Brown.
(She touches his arm.) Dear children, see! His arm.

*(They say "Oh!" in sympathy, and then burst into
ringing cheers—agony of* VALENTINE. PHŒBE, *at*
L.C., *signs to them to go. She shepherds them across
as* SUSAN *stands at the door* R. *When the children
have passed him,* VALENTINE *moves slowly across
up* L.C., *below the settee.* PHŒBE *moves down to* L.
of the desk. SUSAN *closes the door* R., *and crosses
down* L. *to close the door there.)*

VALENTINE *(turning at* C.*).* A terrible ordeal, ma'am.
I think I would be well advised to steal away now,
Miss Phœbe, lest they return in added numbers.

PHŒBE *(*L. *of the desk).* I wish you very happy at
the ball.

VALENTINE *(coming down* C.*).* Miss Susan, cannot
we turn all these maps and horrors out till the vacation
is over?

SUSAN *(moving in to* L.C.*).* Indeed, sir, we always
do. By to-morrow this will be my blue and white room
again. *(Looking* L.*)* And that my sweet spare bedroom.
(She moves up to the settee.)

PHŒBE. For five weeks!

VALENTINE *(*C.*).* And then—the—the dashing Mr.
Brown will drop in as of old and behold Miss Susan
on her knees once more putting tucks into my little
friend, the ottoman, and Miss Phœbe—Miss Phœbe—
(Turning to PHŒBE, *who is* R.*)*

PHŒBE. Phœbe— *(Crossing* L.*)* Phœbe of the ringlets!

(She exits quietly, L.*)*

VALENTINE *(miserably; coming down a little* C.*)*
Miss Susan, what a shame it is.

SUSAN *(hotly)*. Yes, it is a shame!

VALENTINE. The brave Captain Brown! Good God, ma'am, how much more brave are the ladies who keep a school. *(He turns up stage, hearing the door open.)*

(Enter PATTY R., showing in CHARLOTTE PARRATT, a young lady, followed by ENSIGN BLADES, a heavy young soldier. She is very proud of him, and checks just inside the room, to lead him down L. of the desk. She does not see VALENTINE, and crosses to SUSAN at L.C. BLADES, left at down R.C., exchanges recognition with VALENTINE.)

SUSAN *(coming down and meeting her)*. Charlotte Parratt!

(They kiss.)

CHARLOTTE *(turning at L.C.. and sees VALENTINE)*. La! But I did not know you had company, Miss Susan.

SUSAN. 'Tis Captain Brown—Miss Charlotte Parratt.

(VALENTINE comes down.)

CHARLOTTE *(gushing)*. The heroic Brown? *(A low curtsy.)*

VALENTINE *(bowing)*. Alas, no, ma'am—the other one.

(SUSAN motions CHARLOTTE to sit by her on the form up L.C. BLADES has been standing very self-conscious.)

CHARLOTTE *(seated R. of SUSAN)*. Miss Susan, do you see who accompanies me?

SUSAN *(looking across at BLADES)*. I cannot quite recall—

BLADES *(at R.C., bowing)*. A few years ago, ma'am, there sat in this room a scrubby, inky little boy. I was that boy.

SUSAN. Can it be! Our old pupil—Ensign Blades.

(She admires him—he is pleased.)

BLADES. Once a little boy and now your most obedient— *(He bows pompously.)*

SUSAN. You have come to recall old memories?

BLADES. Not exactly—I—I—Charlotte, explain. *(He sits on the form R., indicating to CHARLOTTE to speak.)*

CHARLOTTE. Ensign Blades wishes me to say that it must seem highly romantic to you to have a pupil who has fought at Waterloo.

BLADES. Hah!

SUSAN. Not exactly romantic! I trust sir, that when you speak of having been our pupil you are also so obliging as to mention that it was during our first year. Otherwise it makes us seem so elderly.

BLADES. Excuse me smiling, but I am something of a quiz. Charlotte. *(Meaning, "Continue.")*

(He and CHARLOTTE exchange smiles and VALENTINE stamps his foot angrily at BLADES.)

CHARLOTTE. Ensign Blades would be pleased to hear, Miss Susan, what you think of him as a whole.

(BLADES listens eagerly.)

SUSAN. Indeed, sir. I think you are monstrous fine. *(The light begins to fade, very slowly.)* It quite awes me to remember that we used to whip him.

(BLADES rises.)

VALENTINE *(comes down C., delighted)*. Whipped him. Miss Susan— *(In solemn burlesque of CHARLOTTE.)* Ensign Blades wishes to indicate that it was more than Bonaparte could do. *(He bows to CHARLOTTE and MISS SUSAN who rise and curtsy.)* Ladies!

(Turning to BLADES.*)* We shall meet again, bright boy. *(He slaps* BLADES' *back.)*

*(*VALENTINE *exits* R. BLADES *turns up towards the door —and then faces them.)*

BLADES. Do you think he was quizzing me?
SUSAN. No, indeed.
BLADES *(coming down* R.C.*)*. He said "bright boy," ma'am.

*(*CHARLOTTE *crosses to* BLADES, *as if to reassure him.)*

SUSAN. I am sure, sir, he did not mean it.

(Enter PHŒBE L. *She moves to* C., *holding out both hands.)*

PHŒBE. Charlotte—I am happy to see you. You look delicious, my dear—so young and fresh.
CHARLOTTE *(affectionately taking her hands)*. La! Do you think so? *(She laughs, then turns to glance at* BLADES.*)*
BLADES *(who thinks he is being neglected)*. Miss Phœbe, your obedient. *(He bows.)*
PHŒBE. Ensign Blades! But how kind of you. sir, to revisit the old school.

*(*SUSAN *has seated herself* L.C.*)*

CHARLOTTE *(who has exchanged looks with* BLADES**)**. Ensign Blades has a favour to ask of you, Miss Phœbe.
BLADES *(*R.C.*)*. I learn, ma'am, that Captain Brown has obtained a card for you for the ball, and I am here to solicit for the honour of standing up with you
PHŒBE *(turning and moving a pace* L.C.*)*. Susan, *he* does not think me too old. *(She turns to* BLADES.*)* Sir, I thank you. *(She curtsys to him. Then, raising her eyes, she—and* SUSAN—*intercept a titter between*

CHARLOTTE *and* BLADES. PHŒBE'S *smile freezes.)* Is it—is it only that you desire to make sport of me?

BLADES. Oh no, ma'am, I vow—I—I am such a rattle, ma'am.

PHŒBE. I see!

SUSAN *(rises).* Sister!

(PHŒBE *stops her with a tiny gesture.)*

PHŒBE. I am sorry, sir, to have to deprive you of some entertainment, but I am not going to the ball. *(She goes up* R.C. *to the spinet and sits.)*

SUSAN. Ensign Blades, I bid you adieux.

(BLADES *bows awkwardly, crosses to the door* R. *and turns there.)*

BLADES. If I have hurt Miss Phœbe's feelings, I beg to apologize.

SUSAN *(moving to* C.). *If* you have hurt them! Oh, sir, how is it possible for anyone to be as silly as you seem to be.

BLADES. Charlotte, explain!

(He exits R. CHARLOTTE *goes up towards* SUSAN *and is about to speak.* SUSAN *is too quick for her.)*

SUSAN. Miss Parratt, good-bye. (CHARLOTTE *hesitates a moment. Then she turns and exits* R.. *closing the door.* SUSAN *goes up to the window* C. *After a pause she turns lovingly to* PHŒBE. *But* PHŒBE, *fighting with her pain, plays at first excitedly a gay tune, then slowly then comes to a stop with her head bowed. After a moment, she jumps up, courageously brushes away her distress. gets an algebra from the desk and crosses to the form* L., *and sits. At the window, half turning.)* What book is it, Phœbe?

(A lady in ball dress, and a HUSSAR OFFICER, *cross the street, followed by another gentleman. after a pause.)*

PHŒBE. It is an algebra.

SUSAN *(at the window)*. They are going to the ball. My Phœbe should be going to the ball too. *(Coming down* R.C., *dejectedly, she sits on the form.)*

PHŒBE. You jest, Susan. *(A pause.* SUSAN *watches her read.* PHŒBE *has to wipe away a tear—she wipes the book as if a tear has fallen on it. Suddenly, she rises and gives way to the emotion she has been suppressing ever since the entrance of* VALENTINE. *Rising and leaving the book on the form.)* Oh! I hate him, I hate him! Oh, I could hate him if it were not for his poor hand. *(She moves up* C.)

SUSAN. My dear!

PHŒBE *(turning down to face* SUSAN*)*. He thought I was old, because I am weary, and he should not have forgotten. I am only thirty. *(She goes* R. *and sits by* MISS SUSAN, *plaintively.)* Susan, why does thirty seem so much more than twenty-nine? *(Addressing an imaginary* VALENTINE.*)* Oh, sir, how dare you look so pityingly at me? Is it because I have had to work so hard—is it a crime when a woman works? Because I have tried to be courageous—have I been courageous, Susan?

SUSAN. God knows you have.

(The band is heard, playing very softly, in the distance.)

PHŒBE. But it has given me the headache; it has tired my eyes. *(She rises and moves* L.C.*)* Alas, Miss Phœbe, all your charm has gone, for you have the headache, and your eyes are tired. He is dancing with Charlotte Parratt, now, Susan. "I vow, Miss Charlotte, you are selfish and silly, but you are sweet eighteen." "Oh, la, Captain Brown, what a quiz you are." That delights him, Susan—see how he waggles his silly head.

SUSAN. Charlotte Parratt is a goose.

PHŒBE *(moving to* C.*)* 'Tis what gentlemen prefer, Susan, if there were a sufficient number of geese to go round, no woman of sense would ever get a husband.

(The band becomes louder and then dies away.)
"Charming, Miss Charlotte, you are like a garden—"
(The band stops.) "Miss Phœbe was like a garden once,
but 'tis a faded garden now."

SUSAN. If to be ladylike—

PHŒBE *(slightly R.C.)*. Oh, I am tired of being ladylike. I am a young woman still, and to be ladylike is
not enough. I wish to be bright and thoughtless and
merry. My eyes are tired because for ten years they have
seen nothing but maps and desks. Ten years! Ten years
ago I went to bed a young girl and I woke with this
cap on my head. It is not fair. This is not me, Susan,
this is some other person; I want to be myself. *(She
goes to* SUSAN *and kneels, looking up into her face.)*

SUSAN *(kissing her cap)*. Phœbe, Phœbe, you who
have always been so patient.

PHŒBE. Oh, not always. *(Her head on* SUSAN's *lap,
facing down stage)*. If you only knew how I have re-
belled at times, you would turn from me in horror.

SUSAN. Phœbe!

PHŒBE *(raising her head and looking out front)*.
Susan, I have a picture of myself as I used to be. I
sometimes look at it. I sometimes kiss it, and say "Poor
girl," they have all forgotten you. But I remember.

SUSAN. I do not recall it.

PHŒBE. I keep it locked away in my room. Would
you like to see it? I shall bring it down. *(She rises and
breaks a little C.)*

(She runs off R., leaving the door open. SUSAN, *rises
sadly, and crosses slowly to the form L.C., and sits,
taking up an algebra book. A* LAMPLIGHTER, *with
steps and a lighted torch, passes in the street from
L. to R. He may be seen mounting his steps and lighting a lamp just out of sight, and then disappearing.)*

SUSAN. "A stroke B multiplied by B stroke C equal
A B stroke A little 2 stroke A C add B C" Poor Phœbe—
"multiply C stroke A and we get"— Poor Phœbe—

"C A B stroke A little 2 stroke A C little 2 add B C"—
Oh, I can't believe it.

(Enter PATTY R., *carrying a lamp, turned very low. She takes it to the table up* L.C., *and turns up the wick full, looking at* SUSAN *with affectionate reproach.)*

PATTY *(severely, yet evidently fond of her)*. Hurting your poor eyes, reading without a lamp! Think shame, Miss Susan! *(She crosses up to the windows.)*

SUSAN. Patty, I will not be dictated to! (PATTY *looks out at the street.)* Draw the curtains at once. I cannot allow you to stand gazing at the foolish creatures who crowd to a ball.

PATTY *(closing the casement curtains)*. I'm not looking at them, ma'am, I'm looking for my sweetheart.

SUSAN *(still seated)*. Your sweetheart! *(Softly putting down her book.)* I did not know you had one.

PATTY *(still drawing the curtains)*. Nor have I, ma'am, as yet. But I looks out, and thinks to myself, at any moment he may turn the corner—I ha' been looking out at windows waiting for him to oblige by turning the corner these fifteen years. *(She draws the heavy curtains over the bay.)*

SUSAN. Fifteen years! And you are still hopeful!

PATTY *(giving the curtains a final tug)*. There's not a more hopeful woman in all the King's dominions. *(She comes down* C.)

SUSAN *(looking at her wonderingly)*. You who are so much older than Miss Phœbe.

PATTY. Yes, ma'am, I ha' the advantage of her by five years.

SUSAN. It would be idle to pretend that you are specially comely.

PATTY *(crossing* L., *and looking towards the small mirror on the mantelshelf)*. Well, my face is my own, and the more I see it *(blithely)* the better it pleases me. I never look at it but I says to myself: "Who is to be the lucky man?"

SUSAN. 'Tis wonderful.

PATTY. This will be a great year for females, ma'am. *(As she crosses to* R.C.*)* Think how many of the men who marched away strutting to the wars have come back reflecting that a genteel female is more desirable than glory. *(She turns to* SUSAN *at* C.*)* And who is to teach them that they are right at last? You, ma'am, or me?

SUSAN. Patty!

PATTY *(doggedly)*. Or Miss Phœbe. *(With feeling.)* The pretty thing that she was.

SUSAN. Do you remember, Patty? I think there be no other person who remembers unless it be the Misses Willoughby and Miss Henrietta.

PATTY. Oh, ma'am. *(Eagerly, going to* R. *of* SUSAN.*)* Give her her chance, and take her to the ball. There are to be three of them this week, and the last ball will be the best, for 'tis to be at the barracks, and you will need a carriage to take you there, and there will be the packing of you into it by gallant squires and the unpacking of you out, and other deviltries.

SUSAN *(rising)*. Patty! *(She comes down* L.C.*)*

PATTY *(following down* R. *of* SUSAN*)*. If Miss Phœbe were to dress young again— (SUSAN *sits on the form, facing down* L.*)* and put candles in her eyes that used to be so bright, and coax back her curls—

(PHŒBE *enters* R., *treading softly, carrying a candle, alight. She comes down* L. *of the desk.* SUSAN *is turned a little towards* L. PATTY *stops, amazed by the entrance of* PHŒBE *looking young and beautiful again. She is wearing the wedding gown of Act I. Her ringlets are glorious, her figure youthful, her face flushed and animated—she signs to* PATTY *to go, giving her the candlestick.* PATTY *exits* R., *much impressed.* SUSAN *has not looked round.)*

PHŒBE. Susan! (SUSAN *turns, sees her and is amazed. She rises, quickly. Her arms at her side during*

this speech, looking at the ground, she is very quiet.)
Susan, this is the picture of my old self that I keep
locked away in my room, and sometimes take out of its
box to look at. This is the girl who kisses herself in
the glass and sings and dances with glee—until I put
her away frightened lest you should hear her.

SUSAN. How marvellous! *(She goes to her at c.).*
Oh, Phœbe!

PHŒBE *(very quiet).* Perhaps I should not have done
it, but it is so—easy. I have but to put on the old wedding gown and tumble my curls out of the cap. *(The
band is heard, very softly. Passionately.)* Sister, am I
as changed as he says I am?

SUSAN. You almost frightened me. *(She embraces
PHŒBE.)* Oh, Phœbe!

PHŒBE. Susan! *(Excitedly.)* Susan, let us be happy.
The music is calling to us, dear—I will celebrate Waterloo—in a little ball of my own. See, my curls have begun
to dance—they are so eager to dance. One dance, Susan,
to Phœbe of the ringlets, and then I shall put her away
in her box and never look at her again. *(Like a beau.)*
Ma'am, may I have the honour? Nay, then I shall dance
alone. *(She dances to the music.)*

*(After a few bars she takes SUSAN's hand and they
dance together. Enter PATTY R.)*

PATTY *(astonished).* Miss Phœbe!

PHŒBE *(still dancing).* Not Miss Phœbe, Patty—I
am not myself to-night. I am—let me see, I am my
niece.

PATTY. But Miss Susan, 'tis Captain Brown.

SUSAN. Captain Brown. Oh, stop, Phœbe, stop!

PATTY. No, no, let him see her—let him see her.
*(SUSAN disengages herself, turns and runs off L.
PHŒBE comes down L. PATTY runs over to R., and
announces.)* Captain Brown!

*(Enter VALENTINE R. He comes R.C., carrying a small
phial wrapped in paper in his hand.)*

VALENTINE. I ventured to come back because— *(He stops,* R.C.*)* I beg your pardon, ma'am, I thought it was Miss Susan, or Miss Phœbe.

*(*PHŒBE *is surprised at his mistake, but, on a wild impulse, curtsys as to a stranger, and turns away, smiling.)*

PATTY *(with sudden desire to keep up the joke).* 'Tis my mistresses' niece, sir, who is here on a visit.

VALENTINE *(enlightened).* Ah! Oh yes, I understand. *(He bows gallantly and turns up to* PATTY. *The band is heard again.* PHŒBE *dances to up* L.*)* Patty, I obtained this at the apothecary's for Miss Phœbe's headache. It should be taken at once.

PATTY *(taking it).* Miss Phœbe is lying down, sir.

VALENTINE. Is she asleep?

PATTY. No, sir, I think she is wide awake.

VALENTINE. That may soothe her.

PHŒBE *(below the* L. *end of the settee).* Patty, take it to Aunt Phœbe at once.

*(*PATTY *exits* R., *leaving the door open.* VALENTINE *comes down* R.C. PHŒBE *curtsys again up* L.C.*)*

VALENTINE *(coming* C.—*boldly).* Perhaps I may venture to present myself, Miss—Miss—

PHŒBE *(moving down to him).* Miss—Livvy, sir. *(She curtsys.)*

VALENTINE. I am Captain Brown, Miss Livvy, an old friend of your aunts'.

PHŒBE. I have heard them speak of a dashing Mr. Brown. But I think, sir, you cannot be the same.

VALENTINE *(annoyed quickly).* Why not, ma'am?

PHŒBE *(retreating a step).* I ask your pardon, sir.

(The band is now very faint.)

VALENTINE *(after recovering his composure).* I was

sure you must be related. Indeed, for a moment the likeness—even the voice—

PHŒBE *(pouting).* La, sir, you mean I am like Aunt Phœbe. Everyone says so—and indeed 'tis no compliment. *(She turns a little* L.*)*

VALENTINE. 'Twould have been a compliment once. You must be a daughter of the excellent Mr. James Throssel, who used to reside at Great Buckland?

PHŒBE. He is still there.

VALENTINE. A tedious twenty miles from here as I remember.

PHŒBE. La! I have found the journey a monstrous quick one.

(The band off for two bars, then very softly. PHŒBE dances up C.*)*

VALENTINE *(crossing* L.—*eagerly).* Miss Livvy, you go to the ball? *(He turns at* L., *to face her.)*

PHŒBE *(in an acstasy of longing).* Oh, sir! *(In woe.)* I have no card.

VALENTINEE. I have two cards for your aunts. As Miss Phœbe has the headache, your Aunt Susan must take you to the ball.

PHŒBE *(in ecstasy).* Oh! *(She claps her hands and then—dances to him* L.C.*)* Sir, I cannot control my feet.

VALENTINE. They are already at the ball, ma'am. You must follow them.

PHŒBE. Oh, sir, do you think some pretty gentleman might be partial to me at the ball?

VALENTINE. If that is your wish—

PHŒBE *(moving* C.*).* I long, sir, to inspire frenzy in the breast of the male. *(She clasps her arms to her breast.)* Oh, oh! *(With sudden collapse.)* I dare not go! I dare not! *(Moving down stage* R.C.*)*

VALENTINE *(moving eagerly towards her).* Miss Livvy, I vow—

(Enter SUSAN L., *nervously.)*

SUSAN. What is it?

VALENTINE *(turning to her at* C., *moving a little up stage)*. Miss Susan, I have ventured to introduce myself to your charming niece.

(SUSAN *is taken aback.*)

PHŒBE *(crossing to her at* L.). Aunt Susan, don't be angry with your Livvy, your Livvy, Aunt Susan. This gentleman, he says he is the dashing Mr. Brown—he has cards for us for the ball, Auntie. Of course we cannot go—we dare not go— Oh, Auntie. rush and put on your bombazine. *(She takes her hands—pulling her.)*

SUSAN *(staggered)*. Phœbe— *(She draws back a pace below and to* L. *of* PHŒBE.)

PHŒBE. Aunt Phœbe wants me to go. If I say she does, you know she does. Come—

SUSAN. But my dear, my dear!

PHŒBE *(trying to draw* SUSAN R.). Oh, Auntie, why do you talk so much?

VALENTINE *(eagerly)*. I shall see to it, Miss Susan. that your niece has a charming ball.

PHŒBE. He means he will find me sweet partners. *(She smiles at* VALENTINE.)

VALENTINE. Nay, ma'am, I mean I shall be your partner.

PHŒBE *(turning to* SUSAN, *wickedly)*. Aunt Susan, he still dances.

VALENTINE. *Still*, ma'am?

PHŒBE *(curtsying)*. Oh, sir, you are indeed dashing. *(Seeing he is piqued, speaks with exaggerated remorse.)* Nay, do not scowl, I could not help noticing them.

VALENTINE. Noticing what, Miss Livvy?

PHŒBE. The grey hairs, sir.

VALENTINE. I vow, ma'am, there is not one in my head.

PHŒBE. He is such a quiz. I so love a quiz!

VALENTINE. Then, ma'am, I shall do nothing but quiz you at the ball. *(Entreating.)* Miss Susan, I beg—

SUSAN *(at* L., *agitated).* Oh, sir, dissuade her.

VALENTINE. *(at* C.). Nay, I entreat!

PHŒBE *(betwen them, imploringly).* Auntie!

SUSAN *(taking her up* L.C.). Think, my dear, think, think! We dare not.

PHŒBE *(collapsing).* No, we dare not. I cannot go. *(She sits on the settee, definitely.)*

VALENTINE *(moving up to the* R. *end of the settee).* I do not see—

(The music swells.)

PHŒBE *(definitely).* 'Tis impossible. *(But when* PHŒBE *hears the music, her foot goes restlessly to it.* VALENTINE *beats time to her feet. She springs up, drawing* SUSAN *with her.)* We must, we shall—to the ball, the ball—

(Before SUSAN *can protest,* PHŒBE *seizes her and rushes her off* R., *in a daze.* VALENTINE *watches them off, delighted. The music fades and stops.* VALENTINE *comes down* C., *pulls himself together like one bent on conquest. Then he has a disturbing thought— he touches his hair—gets a small looking-glass from the mantelshelf, puts it on the table* L., *peering into it at his hair and proceeding to pull out his grey hairs one by one. While he is thus occupied* PATTY *shows in* R. HENRIETTA, MISS WILLOUGHBY *and* FANNY— HENRIETTA *wears a veil that conceals her face.* HENRETTA *first to* C. MISS WILLOUGHBY *second at* R.C. *and* FANNY *third down* R. *They stare at him. He pulls out a hair, then he pulls out another. He pulls out a third and they give a little cry—he turns and sees them.* HENRIETTA *pulls a string and the veil opens, going to the two sides like little curtains. This startles* VALENTINE.)

HENRIETTA (*at* C., *politely*). 'Tis but the new veil, sir—there is no cause for alarm.

(PATTY, *grinning, is on the watch at the door* R.)

FANNY (*down* R.). Mary, surely we are addressing the gallant Captain Brown.

VALENTINE (*coming down* L.) It is—the Misses Willoughby and Miss Henrietta. 'Tis indeed a gratification to renew acquaintance with such elegant and respectable females.

(*He bows most ceremoniously. They curtsy, in a like manner.*)

MISS WILLOUGHBY (*curiously*). You have seen Miss Phœbe—?

VALENTINE (*going a little* C.). I have had the honour— (MISS WILLOUGHBY *crosses and sits* L. *on the form, and* HENRIETTA *sits on the form* L.C. FANNY *sits on the form below the desk* R. *Moving to* R.C., *below the spinet.*) Miss Phœbe, I regret to say, is now lying down with the headache. (*They exchange glances which mean that the meeting has been too much for her.* PATTY *suppressing a laugh—goes off* R. *Turning down* R.C.) You do not favour the ball to-night?

(*He looks from one to the other. The ladies look gloomy.*)

FANNY. I confess balls are distasteful to me.

HENRIETTA. 'Twill be a mixed assembly. I am credibly informed that the woolen draper's daughter has obtained a card.

VALENTINE (*gravely*). Good God, ma'am, is it possible?

MISS WILLOUGHBY. We shall probably spend the evening here with Miss Susan at the card-table.

VALENTINE. But Miss Susan goes with me to the ball, ma'am.

ALL. Oh!

(This has a sensational effect on all the ladies.)

VALENTINE. Nay, I hope there be no impropriety? Miss Livvy will acompany her.

MISS WILLOUGHBY *(bewildered)*. Miss Livvy?

VALENTINE. Their charming niece. *(He looks towards the door R., expectantly.)*

(HENRIETTA moves herself to the L. end of the settee. MISS WILLOUGHBY leans towards her. They are excited and puzzled.)

MISS WILLOUGHBY } *(together).*   Niece!
HENRIETTA

(Hearing footsteps, VALENTINE goes to the door.)

FANNY *(to MISS WILLOUGHBY)*. They had not apprised us that they have a visitor. Sister, was this friendly?

(VALENTINE opens the door R. Enter SUSAN in her bombazine and bonnet. The sight of the ladies is a great shock to her. She comes down C.)

MISS WILLOUGHBY *(rising)*. We have but now been advised of your intentions for this evening, Miss Susan.

(VALENTINE comes to below the R. end of the spinet.)

HENRIETTA *(rising, huffily)*. We deeply regret our intrusion.

SUSAN *(nervous and rather dazed)*. Please to be not piqued. 'Twas so—sudden—

MISS WILLOUGHBY. I cannot remember, Susan, that

your estimable brother had a daughter. I thought all the three were sons.

SUSAN *(recklessly)*. Three sons and one daughter. *(Quaking.)* Surely you remember little Livvy, Mary?

MISS WILLOUGHBY *(bluntly)*. No, Susan. I do not.

(The band is heard, very softly. HENRIETTA and FANNY begin to move their feet to the music. but are stopped by a gesture from MISS WILLOUGHBY. SUSAN turns to the window, listening and swaying.)

SUSAN *(terrified)*. I—I must go. I hear Livvy calling. *(She turns R.)*

FANNY *(rising—tartly)*. We are not to see her?

SUSAN. Another time—to-morrow. Pray rest a little before you depart, Henrietta—I—I, Phœbe—Livvy—the headache—

(She is about to go, when PHŒBE enters R., running in gaily in wraps and bonnet. She stops in the doorway, startled at sight of them.)

VALENTINE *(coming towards C. a pace)*. Ah, here is Miss Livvy.   *(WARN Curtain.)*

(They turn to look at her, but before they can see her she quickly pulls the strings of her bonnet, which is like HENRIETTA'S, and it closes over her face like curtains.)

SUSAN. This—this is my niece, Livvy, Miss Willoughby, Miss Fanny Willoughby, Miss Henrietta—

(There are general curtsys—rather cold on the part of the visitors.)

VALENTINE *(coming down between SUSAN and PHŒBE)*. Ladies, excuse my impatience, but—

(MISS WILLOUGHBY *sits suddenly, and stares, rigidly.* HENRIETTA *and* FANNY *also sit.)*

MISS WILLOUGHBY *(in a cold clear voice).* One moment, sir. May I ask, Miss Livvy, how many brothers you have?

PHŒBE. Two!

MISS WILLOUGHBY. I thank you.

(She looks at HENRIETTA, *who, taking the point, gives* SUSAN *a sidelong glance.* SUSAN *gives a little gasp.)*

PHŒBE *(quickly, as* SUSAN *gives her a desperate look).* Excluding the unhappy Thomas. *(She bows her head at the sad remembrance.)*

SUSAN *(this, for her, is an inspiration).* We never mention Thomas.

(The visitors bow. SUSAN *curtsys, and turns to the door* R., *already reached by* VALENTINE, *with* PHŒBE *on his arm.* PHŒBE *exits, followed by* SUSAN. VALENTINE *bows at the door, exits, closing it. The ladies look at one another, scenting a scandal. The door slams off* R. *They all run up to the windows, draw the curtains aside and peep out. Then all retreat, giving the curtains a closing tug. They exchange a glance which shows they all have the same thought, as they come slowly down a little.)*

ALL THREE. What—has Thomas **done?**

QUICK CURTAIN.

ACT THREE

The SCENE *is a tent pavilion used as a card and retiring-room at the officers' ball.*

(See Ground Plan.)

Through an opening at the back of it, made by looping up of the canvas, the dancing is seeen going on in a wooded glade. The band is heard, but not seen. Individual dancers can be identified as they dance past or come to resting in the opening. Most—but not all—of the men are in uniform. The floor is of grass. It is lit with candles or lanterns. There are slits in it R. *and* L., *used as entrances. It contains four card-tables; one* L. *up stage, one* R. *up stage, one* R. *down stage and one down* L.C. *There is a couch* C., *set at a slight angle. A long "rout seat" is set against the* L. *wall.*

When the CURTAIN *rises, the following characters are discovered:*

SUSAN, *sitting at the* R. *end of the couch* C.

CHARLOTTE PARRATT, *sitting above the table down* L.C.

Three young ladies sitting on the "rout seat" L. *They are pretty, but wallflowers. The one at the downstage end is named* HARRIET. SUSAN *is evidently chaperoning them.*

There is an OLD SOLDIER *sitting* L. *of the table down* R., *and a* LADY *sitting on the chair above the same table.*

As the CURTAIN *rises, the music begins. There is a buzz of conversation. An* OFFICER *enters* C., *looks at the three ladies down* L. *and exits* R. *When the dance is*

62

over a LADY *and an* OFFICER *enter* C., *and sit at the table up* L., *and two ladies and a gentleman enter* R., *to the table up* R.

OLD SOLDIER *(laughs, seated* L. *of the* R. *table).* Had I been twenty years younger, Lady Emma, I'd have led you to the altar myself. *(He laughs.)*

HARRIET *(rising and going up* L.C. *a little).* Are we so disagreeable that no one will dance with us? *(Moving a step towards* SUSAN.*)* Miss Susan, 'tis infamous. They have eyes for no one but your horrid niece.

CHARLOTTE *(looking out front).* Miss Livvy has taken Ensign Blades from me.

HARRIET *(turning to* CHARLOTTE*).* If Miss Phœbe were here, I am sure she would not allow her old pupils to be so neglected. *(She moves above the table* L.C., *fanning herself with annoyance. Enter* C., *from* R., LIEUTENANT SPICER. *The ladies become alert. As he enters,* HARRIET *turns to meet him up* C.*)* How do you do, sir?

SPICER *(bowing formally).* Nay, ma'am, how do *you* do? *(Rebuffed,* HARRIET *turns away and sits* L. *He turns* C., *to* SUSAN.*)* May I stand beside you, Miss Susan? *(He moves below the couch,* L. *of* SUSAN.*)*

SUSAN *(annoyed).* You have been standing beside us, sir, nearly all the evening.

SPICER. Indeed, I cannot but be cognizant of the sufferings I cause by attaching myself to you in this unseemly manner. Accept my assurance, ma'am, that you have my deepest sympathy.

SUSAN. Then why do you do it?

SPICER. Because you are her aunt, ma'am. *(The young ladies give vent to half-suppressed murmurs of irritation, and turn away.* CHARLOTTE *rises, and goes up to the entrance* L., *fanning herself, and listening to the band which can now be heard in the distance.)* I shall never leave you—never! *(He turns to the ladies, at* L.*)* It is a scheme of mine by which I am in hopes to soften her heart. *(*SUSAN *faces* R., *fanning herself.* SPICER *moves towards* L.C.*)* I am not clever, ladies, and therefore I had to invent an easy scheme. *(When he has fin-ished this speech, he turns, and crosses to above the* C. *couch, and stands there,* L. *of* SUSAN. *When he speaks again, it is her first intimation that he is so near, and she gives a start.)* Her affection for you, ma'am, is beau-tiful to observe, and if she could be persuaded that I seek her hand from a passionate desire to have you for my Aunt Susan—do you perceive anything hope-ful in my scheme, ma'am? *(He takes a pace nearer, bending over respectfully.)*

SUSAN. No sir, I do not.

*(*SPICER *straightens up and sighs. Enter* BLADES C., *from off* R. *The ladies are again hopeful. He comes down a little* L. *of* C. CHARLOTTE, *turning, comes to his left and a little above him.)*

CHARLOTTE *(cajolingly)*. Ensign Blades, I have not danced with you once this evening.

BLADES *(turning to her)*. Nor I with you, Charlotte. *(*CHARLOTTE *is annoyed and goes down* L. *of the table* L.C., *sitting on the seat below it. He turns from the ladies indifferently—to* SUSAN.) May I solicit of you, Miss Susan, is Captain Brown Miss Livvy's guardian —is he affianced to her?

SUSAN *(firmly)*. No, sir.

(Two ladies and gentlemen who have been at the table up R.C. *rise and exit* C. *to* L.)

BLADES *(below the couch, and* L. *of* SPICER). Then by what right, ma'am, does he interfere? Your elegant niece had consented to accompany me to the shrubbery —to look at the moon—

*(*SUSAN *is horrified.)*

SPICER *(turning up* R.). The moon! *(Overcome with woe.)*

CHARLOTTE *(staring out front)*. The flirt!

(The OLD SOLDIER, *down* R., *turns and listens to this.)*

BLADES. And now Captain Brown forbids it. 'Tis infamous!

HARRIET *(rising from the seat* L.*)*. But you may see the moon from here, sir.

BLADES *(after giving it a glance)*. I believe not, ma'am.

*(*HARRIET *sits again.)*

SUSAN. I am happy Captain Brown forbade her.

BLADES. 'Twas but because he is to conduct her to the shrubbery himself.

HARRIET *(rising again)*. Oh!

BLADES *(turning to her)*. If you say "Oh" in that manner, Miss Harriet, I shall get very angry, I know I shall. *(He goes up* C.*)*

*(*HARRIET *sits. The* OLD SOLDIER *turns back to his lady. Exit* BLADES C. *to* R., *pettishly.* SUSAN *rises, crossing* L.C. *above the table.)*

SUSAN *(looking at the ladies who are reproachful, especially* CHARLOTTE*)*. My dear! Shall I take you to some very agreeable ladies?

CHARLOTTE *(rising, tartly)*. No, you shall not. *(Turning up* C.. R. *of* SUSAN.*)* I am going to the shrubbery to watch Miss Livvy.

SUSAN *(quickly)*. Please not.

CHARLOTTE *(at* C., *facing down)*. My chest is weak. I shall sit among the dew.

SUSAN. Charlotte, you terrify me! *(She hurries* C., *to the couch.)* Please to put this cloak about your shoulders! *(She takes* PHŒBE'S *cloak from the couch.)* Nay, my dear, allow me. *(She moves to* R. *of* CHARLOTTE, *and puts the cloak on her.)*

CHARLOTTE *(over her shoulder—tearfully).* If I perish of cold, Miss Susan, be so kind as to find a cheap little grave for me on which Miss Livvy can dance without inconveniencing herself.

(She turns and exits L., pressing her handkerchief to her lips. SUSAN watches her out. then moves down L.C., R. of the table as PHŒBE enters from R., coming down C. SUSAN turns to her.)

PHŒBE *(in confidential tones, drawing SUSAN to C.).* Susan, another offer—Major Linkwater—stout man, black whiskers, fierce expression—he has rushed away to destroy himself.

OLD SOLDIER *(turning in his chair at the table R., down stage).* Miss Livvy, ma'am, what is this about the moon?

(SPICER, R., comes down above the R. end of the couch, showing annoyance.)

PHŒBE *(looking conscious, she turns to SUSAN).* That reminds me, Aunt Susan, I want my cloak.

SUSAN. I have just lent it to poor Charlotte Parratt.

PHŒBE. Oh, Auntie!

OLD SOLDIER. And now, Miss Livvy can't go to the moon, and she is so fond of the moon.

(PHŒBE does not know what to say, but laughs, then blows a kiss to the OLD SOLDIER, turns and exits up C. The OLD SOLDIER chuckles.)

SPICER *(drawing himself up, coming down to R.C. to the OLD SOLDIER).* Am I to understand, sir, that you are intimating disparagement of the moon? *(The OLD SOLDIER raises his brows. A murmuring of voices is heard off.)* If a certain female has been graciously pleased to signify approval of that orb, any slight cast upon the moon, sir, I shall regard as a personal affront.

OLD SOLDIER. Hoity-toity!
SUSAN. Oh, sirs!

(The murmurs swell, and there is a sudden commotion outside, mingling with the music.)

VALENTINE *(off* R.C.*)*. Stand back, everyone—please to go away. *(The band stops suddenly. The voices fade to silence. All on the stage turn to look up* C., *as* VALENTINE *appears, carrying* PHŒBE *in his arms.* BLADES *is also in attendance. Ladies and gentlemen crowd in behind them. Those who were seated on the stage, have now risen and group* R. *and* L. SUSAN, *very agitated, comes to the couch as* VALENTINE *puts* PHŒBE *on it, where* SPICER *has been arranging the cushions. The crowd follows down, all chattering.* VALENTINE *turns to* SPICER.*)* Dicky, tell them I am a physician, and put them out. *(As* SPICER *goes to obey,* VALENTINE *turns to* BLADES, *on his left.)* Fetch water, someone, and a cordial— *(*BLADES *hurries off* R. VALENTINE *tears feathers out of* HARRIET's *fan, and tickles* PHŒBE *with it.)* —excuse me, ma'am.

*(*SUSAN *is kneeling* L. *of* PHŒBE. SPICER, *having shepherded most of the people off* C., *and closed the exit there, now urges* HARRIET *and the other two young ladies off* L., *and exits with them.)*

SUSAN *(at the couch on her knees* L. *of* PHŒBE*)*. My love, it is Susan, your Susan. Oh, Phœbe, Phœbe!
VALENTINE *(above the couch* C.*)*. Nay, Miss Susan, 'tis useless calling for Miss Phœbe. 'Tis my fault, I should not have permitted her to dance so immoderately. Miss Livvy! *(Going up to* R.*)* Why do they delay with the cordial?

(He puts his head out R. *To* SUSAN's *amazement,* PHŒBE *looks up quickly, waggles a finger at her reassuringly and is down again when* VALENTINE *comes down* R.C.

*She gradually recovers—*SUSAN *rises, below the* L. *end of the couch.)*

PHŒBE *(opening her eyes).* Where am I? Is that you, Aunt Susan? What has happened? *(She sits up at the* L. *end of the couch.)*

VALENTINE *(sitting* R. *of her on the couch).* Nay, you must recline, Miss Livvy. (PHŒBE *does so on his shoulder—she makes a moué at* SUSAN.) You fainted. You have over-fatigued yourself.

PHŒBE *(sitting up straight).* I remember.

(Enter BLADES R. *with a glass of brandy. He comes* C., *behind the couch.)*

VALENTINE. Sip this cordial. *(He tries to take the glass from* BLADES.)

BLADES. By your leave, sir. *(He hands it to* PHŒBE, *who sips, and makes a wry face.)*

VALENTINE. She is in restored looks already, Miss Susan.

PHŒBE. I am quite recovered. Perhaps if you were to leave me now with my aunt—my excellent aunt.

VALENTINE. Be off with you, apple cheeks.

BLADES. Sir, I will suffer no reference to my complexion, and if I mistake not *(moving down* R. *of the couch)* this charming lady was addressing *you!*

PHŒBE *(still seated).* Please, go, both of you.

VALENTINE *(rising).* I shall return soon, Miss Livvy. *(Moving above the couch, he arranges her cushion and pats her forehead to the indignation of* BLADES. *He goes* R., *signalling to* BLADES *to follow. The music is heard, very softly.* BLADES *pats* PHŒBE'S *head—arranges cushion, etc., in imitation of* VALENTINE. *Taking his arm.)* That was quite unnecessary.

(He leads BLADES *off* R.)

PHŒBE *(when they have gone, jumps up, handing*

SUSAN *the glass).* Susan, drink this. I left it for you on purpose. I have such awful information to impart. Drink! *(She goes up* R., *peeps off, to see if the coast is clear—and comes down* C., *to* SUSAN. SUSAN *drinks tremblingly, and puts the glass on the table* L.C. *Moving to* R. *of* SUSAN.) Oh, Susan, Miss Henrietta and Miss Fanny are here!

SUSAN *(looking at* PHŒBE). Here?

PHŒBE *(nodding).* Suddenly my eyes lighted on them. At once I slipped to the ground.

SUSAN *(taking a pace to* PHŒBE). You think they did not see you?

PHŒBE. I am sure of it. They talked for a moment to Ensign Blades, and then turned and seemed to be going towards the shrubbery.

SUSAN. He had told them you were there with Captain Brown.

PHŒBE. I was not. *(Half ashamed, yet gleeful.)* But I was only waiting until Charlotte came back with my cloak. Oh, sister, I am sure they suspect, else why should they be here? They never go to balls.

(BOTH *walk up and down the stage excitedly.*)

SUSAN. They have suspected for a week. Ever since they saw you in your veil, Phœbe, on the night of the first ball. How could they but suspect when they have visited us every day since then and we have always pretended that Livvy has gone out.

PHŒBE. Should they see me it will be idle to attempt to deceive them. *(She turns up* R.)

SUSAN. Idle indeed! Phœbe—the scandal! You—a demure schoolmistress. *(She sits* C.)

PHŒBE *(moving down* R., *distressed).* That is it, sister. A little happiness has gone to my head like strong waters. *(She moves restlessly across to* L.C.)

SUSAN. My dear, stand still, and think.

(PHŒBE *turns.*)

PHŒBE. I dare not—I cannot! Oh, Susan, if they see me we need not open school again! *(She kneels L. of* SUSAN.) Oh, Susan. I know not what I am saying, but you know who it is that has turned me into this wild creature— *(She sobs.)*

SUSAN. Oh, Valentine Brown—how could you!

PHŒBE *(raising her head and turning away).* To weary of Phœbe—to turn from her with a "Bah, you make me old—" and become enamoured in a night of a thing like this! *(She indicates herself.)*

SUSAN. Yes, yes, indeed. *(Then, touching* PHŒBE *with sympathy.)* Yet he has been kind to us. He has been to visit us several times.

PHŒBE *(rising).* In the hope that he would see *her!* *(Facing* SUSAN, L.C.) Was he not most silent and gloomy when we always said she was gone out?

SUSAN. He is infatuate. (PHŒBE *turns away weeping.* SUSAN *hesitates. Then:)* Sister, you are not partial to him still?

PHŒBE. No, Susan, no. *(She comes to* C. *and sits* L. *of* SUSAN.) I did love him all those years, though I never spoke of it to you. I never had any hope—I put that away at once, I folded it up and kissed it and put it away like a pretty garment I could never wear again, but I loved to think of him as a noble man. *(She rises scornfully and goes down* R.) But he is not a noble man, and Livvy found it out in an hour. *(She turns.)* The Gallant! *(Crossing up* L.C., *almost exulantly.)* I flirted that I might enjoy his fury. *(Turning to* SUSAN.) Susan, there has been a declaration in his eyes all to-night, and when he cries: "Adorable Miss Livvy, be mine!" I mean to answer with an "Oh, la, how ridiculous you are! You are much too old—I have been but quizzing you, sir!"

SUSAN. Phœbe, how can you be so cruel?

PHŒBE *(to* C.). Because he has taken from me the one great glory that is in a woman's life. Not a man's love—she can do without that—but her own dear, sweet love for him. He is unworthy of my love, and that is why I can be so cruel.

SUSAN. Oh, dear.

PHŒBE (*to above the chair* R. *of the* L.C. *table*). And now my triumph is to be denied me, for we must steal away home now before Henrietta and Fanny see us.

SUSAN (*rising, and coming forward a little—eagerly*). Yes—yes!

PHŒBE (*sadly*). And to-morrow we must say that Livvy has gone back to her father, for I dare keep up this deception no longer. (*The band is heard, playing very softly.*) Come, Susan. (*She moves up towards the* C. *opening.*)

SUSAN (*with a gesture to check* PHŒBE). Those gentlemen would not let you go. Not that way—

(*She goes to the opening* R., *sees* FANNY, *off stage, and starts back.* PHŒBE *sees this and comes down a little.*)

PHŒBE (C.). What is it?

SUSAN (*turning, agitated*). Miss Fanny—she is coming here.

(*She signs to* PHŒBE. *They both turn and run to the* L. *exit—*PHŒBE *first—but she starts back.*)

PHŒBE (L., *distressed*). Susan—'tis Henrietta!

SUSAN (L.C., *panic-striken*). We are lost!

PHŒBE (*coming down* L.). Sit down quickly. (SUSAN *goes to the couch* C. *and sits. Drawing the chair above the* L.C. *table out a little.*) Susan, bear up! I will confess all to them—and beg for mercy. (*She sits.*)

(FANNY *and* HENRIETTA *peep in at the openings* R. *and* L. *They observe* SUSAN *and* PHŒBE, *and then enter, moving down* R. *and* L.)

HENRIETTA (*coming down* L, *surprised and gazing*

in amazement, evidently not having expected to find
PHŒBE *here*). You, Miss Phœbe!

PHŒBE *(shrinking)*. Yes.

HENRIETTA. What a wonderous change! You are
scarce knowable.

FANNY *(down R., also amazed)*. How amazing! You
do not deny, ma'am, that you are Miss Phœbe?

PHŒBE *(humbly)*. Yes, Fanny, I am Miss Phœbe.

(FANNY *and* HENRIETTA *look at each other perplexed
and begin to tremble, ashamed.*)

HENRIETTA *(going on one knee L. of PHŒBE and
taking her hand)*. Miss Phœbe, we have done you a
cruel wrong.

FANNY *(coming timidly to L.C.)*. Phœbe, we apologize. *(Above and to R. of the table.)*

(PHŒBE *is bewildered as she was just about to apologize. She glances from one to the other.*)

HENRIETTA. Oh dear, to think how excitedly we have
been following her about in the shrubbery.

FANNY. She is wearing your cloak.

PHŒBE *(beginning to understand)*. Cloak! *(She
rises.)*

HENRIETTA *(rising and retreating a pace up L.)*.
Ensign Blades told us she was gone to the shrubbery.

(PHŒBE *moves down L. of the table to below it, looking at FANNY.*)

FANNY. And we were convinced there was no such
person. *(She turns up to the opening C.)*

(PHŒBE *looks at* HENRIETTA.)

HENRIETTA *(coming down level with PHŒBE)*. So
of course we thought it *must* be you.

(PHŒBE *sits below the table on the seat, staring out front.*)

FANNY *(looking out, to* L.). I can discern her in the shrubbery still. She is decidedly shorter than Phœbe.

HENRIETTA. I thought she looked shorter. I meant to say so, Phœbe—'twas the cloak deceived us—we could not see her face.

(FANNY *comes down to* R. *of* PHŒBE. SUSAN *is dazed.*)

PHŒBE *(beginning to understand).* Cloak! You mean, Miss Henrietta—you mean, Fanny—

FANNY *(kneeling by* PHŒBE). 'Twas wicked of us, my dear, but we—we thought that you and Miss Livvy were the same person.

(SUSAN *rises, coming down a pace.*)

PHŒBE *(silencing* SUSAN *with a look—indignant).* What! Susan!

HENRIETTA *(to* SUSAN). Miss Susan, plead for us. *(To* PHŒBE). Phœbe. forgive!

FANNY. Phœbe, pardon, pardon!

(PHŒBE *is obdurate, as* HENRIETTA, L. *of her, and* FANNY, R. *of her, fall weeping on* PHŒBE'S *knee,* PHŒBE *quickly motions* SUSAN *to go.* SUSAN *goes off* R. *quickly. Then* HENRIETTA *raises her head and speaks.*)

HENRIETTA. Oh, my love, if you knew how many rabbit-holes I fell into.

PHŒBE *(graciously pardoning).* Poor Henrietta!

FANNY. Phœbe, you look so pretty. Are they paying you no attention, my dear?

PHŒBE *(to* FANNY). They think of none but Livvy. They come to me only to tell me that they adore her.

HENRIETTA. Surely not Captain Brown.
PHŒBE. He is infatuate about her.
HENRIETTA. Oh!
FANNY. Poor Phœbe!

(To the alarm of PHŒBE, *who rises and runs to* L., *with her back to him, enter* BLADES R. *He comes down* R.C. HENRIETTA *and* FANNY *rise, the latter moving up to* R. *of the table.)*

HENRIETTA *(crossing to* L. *of* BLADES*)*. Mr. Blades, I have been saying if I were a gentleman I would pay my addresses to Miss Phœbe much rather than to her niece.
BLADES. Ma'am, excuse me!
HENRIETTA *(indignantly)*. Sir, you are a most ungallant and deficient young man!
BLADES *(roused)*. Really, madam, I assure you—
HENRIETTA. Not another word, sir.

*(*BLADES *turns away to face down* R., *fuming.)*

PHŒBE *(crossing up, behind* HENRIETTA *to below the* L. *end of the couch* C.*)*. Leave him to me, Miss Fanny, Miss Henrietta. It is time I spoke plainly to this gentleman. *(She sits on the couch* C.. *facing* L.*)*
BLADES *(turning)*. I swear, ma'am—
HENRIETTA *(turning her back on* BLADES*)*. Indeed my dear, we applaud your courage. *(She goes up and presses* PHŒBE'S *hand.)*
PHŒBE. What I have to say had best be said to him alone.
FANNY *(up to* L. *of* PHŒBE*)*. If we could remain—
PHŒBE. Would it be seemly, Fanny?
HENRIETTA. Come, Fanny. *(*FANNY *goes up.* HENRIETTA *follows, checking* R. *of the table up* L.*)* Sir, you bring your punishment upon yourself.

*(*FANNY *and* HENRIETTA *exit up* C. PHŒBE *rises taking a pace down* C.*)*

BLADES *(moving to* R. *of* PHŒBE*)*. Punishment! Miss Livvy! (PHŒBE *flicks her fan in imitation of the cane, and then advances on him and he retreats a pace or two.)* Are you angry with me, Miss Livvy?

PHŒBE *(relieved of anxiety, and careless)*. Oh, no! *(She laughs, sits and motions him to sit* R. *of her, moving to the* L. *end of the couch.)* Sit down, bright sir. *(Her foot waggles a little.)*

(BLADES *moves to below the* R. *end of the couch.)*

BLADES. Miss Livvy, I have something to say to you of supreme importance to both of us. Before I say it, be so good as not to waggle your foot—it fidgets me.

PHŒBE. I shall sit still.

BLADES *(sitting* R. *of* PHŒBE*)*. With regard to my complexion. I am aware, Miss Livvy, my complexion has retained a too youthful bloom. My brother officers comment on it with a certain lack of generosity. *(Anxiously.)* Might I inquire, madam, whether you regard my complexion as a subject for light talk?

PHŒBE. No, indeed, sir, I only wish I had it.

BLADES. Miss Livvy, ma'am, you may have it.

(Enter SPICER C. *from* R., *jealously.)*

SPICER *(coming down* L.C., *quite close to* PHŒBE*)*. It is my dance, Miss Livvy—not Ensign Blades'.

BLADES *(rising)*. Leave us, sir! His affection, Miss Livvy, is not so deep as mine. He is a light and shallow nature.

PHŒBE *(in an outburst)*. You are both light and shallow natures.

BLADES *(backing a pace or two down* R.*)*. Both, ma'am!

PHŒBE. Oh, 'tis such as you with your foolish flirting ways that confuse the minds of women and make us try to be as silly as yourselves.

SPICER *(*L., *backing away, blandly)*. Ma'am!

PHŒBE. I did not mean to hurt you. *(They sulk.)* You are so like little boys in a school! *(Cajoling, treating them as children.)* Do be good. Sit here. *(She beckons both, with her fingers.)* I know you are very brave—

(SPICER joyfully sits L. of her.)

BLADES. Hah! *(He sits, gratified, on her R.)*
PHŒBE. And when you come back from the wars it must be so delightful to flirt with the ladies again.
SPICER. Oh, ma'am.
PHŒBE. As soon as you see a lady with a pretty nose you cannot help saying that you adore her.
BLADES. Hah!

(SPICER giggles.)

PHŒBE. 'Tis our noses that undo us. You feel compelled to say you love us merely because you are so deficient in conversation.

(SPICER giggles again.)

BLADES. Charming, Miss Livvy!

(They each take a hand.)

PHŒBE *(irritated)*. Oh, sir, go away—go away, both of you, I weary of you exceedingly—go away— *(She throws away their hands. BLADES and SPICER rise and go up R. and L., respectively.)* —and read improving books.

(Enter VALENTINE C., annoyed to see them.)

VALENTINE *(up L.C.)*. Gentlemen, I instructed this lady to rest, and I am surprised to find you in attendance. *(He comes below the couch, L. of PHŒBE.)* Miss

Livvy, you must be weary of their fatuities, and I have
taken the liberty to order your chaise.

PHŒBE *(haughtily)*. It is indeed a liberty. *(She
rises.)*

BLADES. An outrage! *(He comes down* R.)

PHŒBE. I prefer to remain.

VALENTINE. Nay.

PHŒBE. I promised this dance to Ensign Blades.

SPICER *(coming down* L.C., *above the table)*. To me,
ma'am.

PHŒBE. And to you the next. *(To* BLADES.) Your
arm, sir. *(She takes his arm.)*

VALENTINE. I forbid any further dancing.

PHŒBE. Forbid! La!

BLADES. Sir, by what right—

VALENTINE. By a right which I hope to make clear
to Miss Livvy as soon as you gentlemen have retired.

*(*PHŒBE *disengages from* BLADES *and comes* C.)*

PHŒBE *(thinking the declaration is coming)*. I am
curious to know what Captain Brown can have to say
to me. *(To* BLADES *and* SPICER *in turn.)* In a few
minutes—Mr. Blades, Lieutenant Spicer—I shall be at
your service.

VALENTINE. I trust not. *(He puts his helmet on the
table* L.C., *and returns to* C., *below* L. *end of the couch.)*

PHŒBE *(to* BLADES *and* SPICER). I give you my
word. *(She curtsys.)*

*(*BLADES *and* SPICER *bow to her.* SPICER *crosses* R. *to*
BLADES *and they exit* R. *The band stops.* VALEN-
TINE *moving a little down* L.C., *speaks half-scolding,
half-humorously.)*

VALENTINE. You are an amazing pretty **girl, ma'am**,
but you are a shocking flirt.

PHŒBE *(turning down* R.C.). La!

VALENTINE. It has somewhat diverted me to watch

them go down before you *(kindly)*, but I know you have a kind heart, and that if there be a rapier in your one hand there is a handkerchief in the other ready to staunch their wounds. *(He bows.)*

PHŒBE *(contemptuously—facing him)*. I have not observed that they bled much. *(She curtsys.)*

VALENTINE. The Blades and the like—no. But one may perhaps.

PHŒBE *(harshly, crossing up to the couch)*. Perhaps I may *wish* to see *him* bleed. *(She sits facing* R.)

VALENTINE *(up to this time he has been kindly— now stern)*. For shame! Miss Livvy! I speak, ma'am, in the interests of the man to whom I hope to see you affianced.

*(*PHŒBE *falters and, wishing to avow the proposal, makes as if to rise.)*

PHŒBE. No, I have changed my mind, I shall go home. I—

VALENTINE *(with a restraining gesture)*. Nay.

PHŒBE *(rising; turns, almost coaxing)*. I beg you—

VALENTINE. No. We must have this out.

PHŒBE *(coldly)*. Then if you must go on, do so. *(She turns her face away.)* But remember I begged you to desist. *(She sits* C.) Who is this happy man? *(Smiling.)*

VALENTINE *(moving to above the* L. *end of the couch)*. As to whom he is, ma'am, of course I have no notion. *(The shock to* PHŒBE *is unseen by him.)* Nor, I am sure, have you. *(In a kindly way.)* Else you would be more guarded in your conduct. But some day, Miss Livvy, the right man will come. Not to be able to tell him all—would it not be hard? And how could you acquaint him with this poor sport? His face would change, ma'am, as you told him of it, and yours would be a false face until it was told. *(He speaks this in a kind fatherly manner—she is crushed.)* This is what

I have been so desirous to say to you—by the right of
a friend.

Phœbe (*with her head down*). I see.

Valentine (*moving a little* L.). It has been hard to
say and I have done it bunglingly. (*Coming back to*
L.C.) Ah, but believe me, Miss Livvy, it is not the
flaunting flower men love—it is the modest violet.

Phœbe. The modest violet—*you* dare to say that!

Valentine. Yes, indeed, and when you are acquaint
with what love really is—

Phœbe (*scornfully*). Love! What do you know of
love?

Valentine (*complacently, wagging his head*). Why,
ma'am, I know all about it! (*Half smiling to himself.*)
I am in love, Miss Livvy! (*Emphatic, half-humorously.*)

Phœbe (*amazed, pauses, then:*) I wish you very
happy.

Valentine. With a lady who was once very like you,
ma'am.

(*The band is heard, playing very softly. At this* Phœbe
*does not understand; then a suspicion of his meaning
comes to her.*)

Phœbe (*startled*). Not—not— (*Feeling it can't be.*)
Oh no!

Valentine. I had not meant to speak of it, but
why should not I? It will be a fine lesson to you, Miss
Livvy. Ma'am, it is your Aunt Phœbe whom I love.

Phœbe (*rigidly*). You do not mean that!

Valentine. Most ardently. (*He goes to the table*
L.C. *and sits on it.*)

Phœbe. It is not true—how dare you make sport of
her!

Valentine. Is it sport to wish she may be my wife?

Phœbe. Your wife?

Valentine. If I could win her.

(Phœbe *is in rapture—but instantly controls it.*)

PHŒBE *(with apparent composure).* May I solicit, sir, for how long you have been attached to Miss Phœbe?

VALENTINE. For nine years, I think.

PHŒBE *(bitterly).* You think!

VALENTINE *(like one puzzled over it himself).* I want to be honest. Never in all that time had I thought myself in love. Your aunts were my dear friends, and while I was at the wars we sometimes wrote to each other, but they were only friendly letters; I presume the affection was too placid to be love.

PHŒBE. I think that would be Aunt Phœbe's opinion.

VALENTINE *(musing).* Yet I remember, before we went into action for the first time—I suppose the fear of death was upon me—some of them were making their wills—I have no near relative—I left everything to these two ladies.

PHŒBE *(very softly).* Did you?

VALENTINE. And when I returned a week ago and saw Miss Phœbe—grown so tired-looking, and so poor—

PHŒBE. The shock made you feel old—I know!

VALENTINE. No, Miss Livvy, but it filled me with a sudden passionate regret that I had not gone down in that first engagement. They would have been very comfortably left.

PHŒBE *(trying to keep her voice steady).* Oh, sir.

VALENTINE. I am not calling it love.

PHŒBE. It was sweet and kind, but it was not love.

VALENTINE *(decisively).* It is love now. *(He rises and goes to her.)*

PHŒBE. No, it is only pity.

VALENTINE. It is love.

(All that PHŒBE feels for the moment is the rapture that it is her real self who is loved. It is the one thing she wants to be sure of. She gazes out front—then half turning towards him, fearing it is too glorious to be true.)

PHŒBE. You really mean Phœbe—tired, unattractive Phœbe. (VALENTINE *makes a gesture of disgust, standing.*) That woman whose girlhood is gone! Nay, impossible!

VALENTINE *(stoutly, moving up* C., *on her* L.). Phœbe of the fascinating playful ways, whose ringlets were once as pretty as yours, ma'am. I have visited her in her home several times this week—you were always out— I thank you for that. *(He bows.)* I was alone with her— and with fragrant memories of her.

PHŒBE. Memories! Yes, that is the Phœbe you love —the bright girl of the past—not the schoolmistress in her old maid's cap!

VALENTINE. There you wrong me, for I have discovered for myself that the schoolmistress in her old maid's cap is the noblest Miss Phœbe of them all. *(He turns a little* L. PHŒBE *is in ecstasy.)* When I enlisted I remember I compared her to a garden. I have often thought of that.

PHŒBE. 'Tis an old garden now.

VALENTINE. The paths, ma'am, are better shaded.

PHŒBE. The flowers have grown old-fashioned.

VALENTINE They smell the sweeter. *(The ecstasy of* PHŒBE *is mingled with woe. He goes and sits on her left, impulsively.)* Miss Livvy, tell me, do you think there is any hope for me?

PHŒBE *(controlling herself, looking straight before her).* There was a man whom Miss Phœbe loved— long ago. He did not love her.

(The band stops.)

VALENTINE. Now here was a fool!

PHŒBE. He kissed her once. *(Looking straight before her.)*

VALENTINE If Miss Phœbe suffered him to do that she thought he loved her.

PHŒBE. Yes, yes. *(Pleadingly.)* Do you opinion that

that makes her action in allowing it less reprehensible? It has been such pain to her ever since.

VALENTINE *(smiling fondly)*. How like Miss Phœbe! *(Sternly facing her.)* But that man was a knave!

PHŒBE. No—he was a good man—only a little—inconsiderate—she knows now that he has even forgotten he did it. I suppose men are like that.

VALENTINE. No, Miss Livvy, men are not like that. *(Turning front.)* I am a very average man, but I thank God I am not like that.

PHŒBE *(turning to him, suddenly facing him quickly)*. It was you!

VALENTINE *(after a pause he looks at her)*. Did Miss Phœbe say that?

PHŒBE. Yes.

VALENTINE. Then it is true. *(He is very grave and quiet and turns front.)*

PHŒBE. It was raining and her face was wet. You said you did it because her face was wet.

VALENTINE *(pauses, his head bowed)*. I had quite forgotten.

PHŒBE *(bitterly)*. But she remembers, and how often do you think the shameful memory has made her face wet since? The face you love, Captain Brown, you were the first to give it pain. The tired eyes—how much less tired they might be if they had never known you. You, who are torturing me with every word, what have you done to Miss Phœbe? You who think you can bring back the bloom to that faded garden and all the pretty airs and graces that fluttered round it once like little birds before the nest is torn down— Bring them back to her if you can, sir, it was you who took them away.

VALENTINE *(looking before him)*. I vow I shall do my best to bring them back. *(Rising—hopefully.)* Miss Livvy, with your help— *(Turning to her at L.C.)*

PHŒBE. My help! I have not helped! I tried to spoil it all.

VALENTINE *(humorously)*. To spoil it. You mean that

you sought to flirt even with me! Oh, I knew you did. *(Lightly.)* But that is nothing.

PHŒBE *(turning round entreatingly, rapidly)*. Oh, sir, if you could overlook it.

VALENTINE *(freely)*. I do.

PHŒBE *(greatly relieved)*. And forget these hateful balls!

VALENTINE. Hateful! *(As he crosses down R.)* Nay, I shall never call them that. They have done me too great a service. *(He faces front.)* It was at the balls that I fell in love with Miss Phœbe.

PHŒBE *(rising, startled)*. What can you mean?

VALENTINE. She who was never at a ball. *(Implying "Isn't it wonderful?" with sudden humour and horror.)* But I must not tell you—it might hurt you.

PHŒBE *(strongly)*. Tell me. *(She moves down to the chair R. of the L.C. table.)*

VALENTINE. Then on your own head be the blame. *(He moves C., below the couch.)* It is you who have made me love her, Miss Livvy.

PHŒBE. Sir?

VALENTINE *(sits C.)*. Yes, it is odd and yet very simple. You who so resembled her as she was, for an hour, ma'am, you bewitched me, yes, I confess it— *(spoken lightly)* but 'twas only for an hour. How like, I cried at first but soon it was how unlike. There was almost nothing she would have said that you said; you did so much that she would have scorned to do. *(With humorous horror.)* But I must not say these things to you.

PHŒBE. I ask it of you. *(She sits R. of the table.)*

VALENTINE. Well! Miss Phœbe's lady-likeness on which she set such store, that I used to make merry of the word—I gradually perceived that it is a woman's most beautiful adornment, and the casket which contains all the adorable qualities that go to the making of a perfect female. When Miss Livvy rolled her eyes —oh—oh! *(He rises and goes up L.C.)*

PHŒBE *(determined to know the worst)*. Proceed, sir.

VALENTINE *(turning down* C. *again)*. It but made me the more complacent that never in her life had Miss Phœbe been guilty of the slightest deviation from the strictest propriety. *(This is emphatic.* PHŒBE *shudders. Moving down* R.C. *and turning.)* I was always conceiving her in your place— (PHŒBE *half turns to him.)* —oh, it was monstrous unfair to you—I stood looking at you, Miss Livvy, and seeing in my mind *her,* and all the pretty things she did, and you did not do; why, ma'am, that is how I fell in love with Miss Phœbe at the balls. *(He bows.)*

(A pause. PHŒBE *is like one who has heard her doom pronounced. Though agitated during his speech, she is now quiet.)*

PHŒBE *(dully)*. I thank you! *(She rises, crosses to the couch and sits.)*

VALENTINE *(sitting on her* R.*)*. Ma'am, tell me, do you think there is any hope for me?

PHŒBE. Hope?

VALENTINE *(looking at her almost as if meaning it for her)*. I shall go to her, "Miss Phœbe," I will say— oh, ma'am, so reverently—"Miss Phœbe, my beautiful, most estimable of women, let me take care of you for evermore."

*(*PHŒBE *hugs the words to her and then, as it were, lets them fall.)*

PHŒBE *(heartbroken, affecting amusement)*. Ha, beautiful! Aunt Phœbe! *(She laughs.)*

VALENTINE. Ah, you may laugh at a rough soldier so much enamoured, but 'tis true. "Marry me, Miss Phœbe," I shall say—"and I will take you back through those years of hardships that have made your sweet eyes too patient. Instead of growing older you shall grow younger. We will travel back together to pick up the many little joys and pleasures you had to pass by when you trod that thorny path alone."

PHŒBE. Cannot be—cannot be!

VALENTINE. Nay, Miss Phœbe has loved me. 'Tis you have said it.

PHŒBE. I did not mean to tell you.

VALENTINE. She will be my wife yet.

PHŒBE *(rising, she goes down* R.*)*. Never! Never!

VALENTINE *(rises)*. You are severe, Miss Livvy. But it is because you are partial to her, and I am happy of that.

PHŒBE. I am partial to her. I am laughing at both of you. Aunt Phœbe. La, that old thing.

VALENTINE (R.C., *sternly)*. Silence!

PHŒBE. I hate and despise her. If you only knew what she is.

VALENTINE *(sternly)*. I know what you are.

PHŒBE. That paragon who has never been guilty of the slightest deviation from the strictest propriety.

VALENTINE. Never!

PHŒBE. That garden!

VALENTINE. Miss Livvy, for shame!

PHŒBE. Your garden has been destroyed, sir—the weeds have entered it and all the flowers are choked.

VALENTINE. You false woman, what do you mean?

PHŒBE *(facing him recklessly)*. I shall tell you. (VALENTINE'S *proud confidence awes her.* PHŒBE *pauses, then moves towards him.)* What faith you have in her. *(WARN Curtain.)*

VALENTINE. As in my God! Speak!

PHŒBE. I cannot tell you.

VALENTINE. No, you cannot.

PHŒBE. It is too horrible.

VALENTINE. You are too horrible. Is not that it?

PHŒBE. Yes, that is it.

(In agony she turns away. Enter SUSAN R. *in time to hear the last words. She comes* C., *above the couch.)*

SUSAN (*looking from one to the other*). What is too horrible?

(*The band is heard playing.* PHŒBE *can say nothing. She goes to the table down* R. *as* VALENTINE *goes* L.C., *taking his helmet from the table.*)

VALENTINE (*moving up* L.C. *to the* C. *exit*). Ma'am, I leave the telling of it to her—if she dare. (*Turning at the exit.*) And I devoutly hope those are the last words I shall ever address to this lady.

(*He bows and exits stiffly* C. *to* R. SUSAN *goes up* C. *bewildered, then turns down stage* L. *of the couch.*)

SUSAN. My love—my dear, what terrible thing has he said to you?

PHŒBE (*turning to* SUSAN, *suddenly changing to rapture. She flings out her arms.*) Not terrible— glorious, Susan, 'tis Phœbe he loves, 'tis me, not Livvy. (*The music off stage swells. Moving to* SUSAN.) He loves me! He loves me! Me! Phœbe!

(*They embrace.*)

QUICK CURTAIN.

ACT FOUR

The SCENE *is as in Act I—i.e., the maps, desk, etc., are gone, and the room is entirely the pretty, prim parlour again. The room* L. *is once more a bedroom.*

SUSAN *and* PHŒBE *are discovered sitting apart.* PHŒBE *is seated on the settee down* R., *sadly looking at footlights.* SUSAN *is seated at the fireplace, also looking front very gloomily. The door* L. *is shut.* PHŒBE *is wearing a cap again, her curls hidden away, and once more looks the old maid of the beginning of Act II. They sit looking straight before them and are the picture of woe.*

> *Enter* PATTY R. *She has the demure airs of a servant in the family secrets.*

PATTY (R.). Miss Willoughby.

(The sisters exchange a look of terrible meaning. MISS WILLOUGHBY *enters.* SUSAN *rises—*PHŒBE *turns to* MISS WILLOUGHBY *as she comes to* C., *carrying a bowl with a white cloth over it. She curtsys to* PHŒBE *and crosses to* R. *of* SUSAN.)

MISS WILLOUGHBY. I am just run across, Susan, to inquire how Miss Livvy does now?

*(*PHŒBE *is in the depths and* SUSAN *has to do most of the talking.)*

SUSAN (L.). She is still very poorly, Mary.

87

(They all look at the door L., *with expressions of commiseration.)*

MISS WILLOUGHBY. Dear, dear! I conceive it to be a nervous disorder.

SUSAN *(almost too glibly).* Accompanied by trembling, fluttering and spasms. Is it not, Phœbe?

PHŒBE *(turning to front).* Indeed it is.

*(*MISS WILLOUGHBY *believes their story, but is also sure there is something concealed from her.)*

MISS WILLOUGHBY *(with a tentative step* L.) May I go in to see her?

SUSAN *(taking a step down stage between* MISS WILLOUGHBY *and the door* L.). I fear not; she requires complete rest, Mary. *(Going to the door* L., *calling into the room without putting her head in.)* Lie quite still, Livvy, my love, quite still.

(Exit PATTY, *giggling* R. MISS WILLOUGHBY *gives a sigh of disappointment.)*

MISS WILLOUGHBY *(turning to* PHŒBE*).* This is a little arrowroot of which I hope Miss Livvy will be so obliging as to partake.

SUSAN *(taking the bowl promptly, coming to* C. *for it).* I thank you, Mary.

PHŒBE *(disturbed).* Susan, we ought not—

SUSAN. I shall take it to her while it is still warm.

(She exits L., *sniffing pleasantly.* PHŒBE *goes a little up* R.C., *and turns. Her agitation has increased* MISS WILLOUGHBY'S *suspicions.)*

MISS WILLOUGHBY *(going to her* R.C.—*sternly).* Miss Phœbe, why is it that we are not allowed to see Miss Livvy? Has Captain Brown been apprised of her illness?

PHŒBE. She declines to see any physician.

MISS WILLOUGHBY. Is this right, Phœbe? You informed Fanny and Henrietta at the ball of his partiality for Livvy. *(She puts her hand on* PHŒBE'S *shoulder.)* My dear, it is hard for you, I know, but have you any right to keep them apart?

PHŒBE. Is that what I am thought to be doing. Miss Willoughby? *(She crosses to* L.C.)

MISS WILLOUGHBY *(moving a little down* R.). Such a mysterious illness, and the curtains of the sick-room and this room kept drawn so artfully. *(There is a faint insinuation in her tone.)*

*(*SUSAN *peeps in without seeing* MISS WILLOUGHBY.)*

SUSAN. Is she gone? *(She sees* MISS WILLOUGHBY. *She hastily hides the bowl* L. *of her.)*

MISS WILLOUGHBY *(turning: huffily).* No, Susan, but I am going.

(She goes up to the door R., *casts them a hurt glance and exits.)*

SUSAN (C., *distressd).* Mary! *(The door closes.* SUSAN *turns and sits on the settee at the fireplace.* PHŒBE *sits* L.C. *They look at each other; then* SUSAN *who has the bowl in her hand. sits down to it at the fire and sups with avidity, though a little ashamed.* PHŒBE'S *head sinks.)* My dear, I am well aware that this is wrong of me, but Mary's arrowroot is so delicious. *(She sups.)* The ladies' fingers and petticoat tails those officers sent to Livvy, I ate them also. *(*PHŒBE *breaks down with a little moan.)* Phœbe, if you have such remorse you will weep yourself to death!

PHŒBE. Oh, sister, were it not for you how gladly would I go into a decline.

SUSAN. My dear, what is to be done about her?

(Finishing the arrowroot.) Delicious! We cannot have her supposed to be here for ever.

(They both look at the door L., guiltily.)

PHŒBE. We had to pretend that she was ill to keep her from sight, and now we cannot say she has gone home, for the Misses Willoughby's windows command our door, and they are always watching.

*(*SUSAN *rises, puts the bowl on the table and moves to the window.)*

SUSAN. Fanny is watching now. I cannot see her, but I know she is there, by a slight movement of the window curtain. I feel, Phœbe, as if Livvy really existed. *(Coming down* C.*)*

PHŒBE *(earnestly)*. Susan, I meant no enormity. He was so easily deceived, I could not resist the humour of it at first. *(Weeping.)* I had not been humorous for such a long time.

SUSAN *(sympathetically)*. You have such an aptitude for humour, dearest. *(She sits on the settee,* R. *of* PHŒBE.*)*

PHŒBE *(dabbing her eyes)*. I think 'tis one of the great causes of unhappiness that gentlemen will not understand how humorous ladies can be.

SUSAN *(nervously, yet daring)*. Phœbe, why not marry him? If only we could make him think that Livvy had gone home, then he need never know.

PHŒBE *(sternly)*. Get thee behind me, Satanus! She who married without telling all, hers must ever be a false face.

(Enter PATTY R.*)*

PATTY *(a little excited)*. Captain Brown!

(They start.)

PHŒBE *(rising quickly and moving down* R.*)*. I wrote to him begging him not to come. *(She sits on the settee* R.C.*)*

(VALENTINE *appears in the doorway.*)

SUSAN *(still seated* C.*, quickly—not seeing him)*. Patty, I am sorry. but we are gone out.

(VALENTINE *enters just in time to hear these words.*)

VALENTINE *(half amused, ignoring both of them)*. I regret that they are gone out, Patty, but I shall await their return. *(He comes to the ottoman and sits* R. *of* SUSAN *as if she were not there.* PATTY *is giggling. The ladies are horrified, but do not look at* VALENTINE.*)* It is not my wish to detain you, Patty.

(Exit PATTY R.*, disappointed.* VALENTINE *stretches himself as if prepared for a long wait, then hums a tune.)*

SUSAN *(thinking aloud)*. Always so amusing.
PHŒBE *(without rising, timidly)*. Captain Brown.
VALENTINE *(rising)*. Miss Phœbe! it is you. *(He bows.)* I hear Miss Livvy is indisposed.
PHŒBE. She is—in some pain.
VALENTINE. I deeply regret, but a little pain may' do Miss Livvy good, and it is not that unpleasant girl I have come to see, it is you. *(He sits again, with his back to* SUSAN.*)*
SUSAN *(apologetically)*. Captain Brown—
VALENTINE *(ignoring her and addressing* PHŒBE*)*. And I am happy to find you alone.
SUSAN. —how do you do, sir?
PHŒBE. You know quite well, sir, that Susan is here.
VALENTINE. Nay, ma'am, excuse me. I heard Miss

Susan say she was gone out— (SUSAN *rises.*) Miss Susan is incapable of prevarication.

SUSAN *(disturbed, going down* L. *to the door, addressing vacancy).* What am I to do?

PHŒBE *(anxiously).* Don't go, Susan—'tis what he wants!

VALENTINE. I have her word that she is not present.

SUSAN. Oh, dear!

VALENTINE. My faith in Miss Susan is absolute.

(Exit SUSAN L., *pleased with this remark. She closes the door.* VALENTINE *looks* L., *bows to the door, without rising, then he looks at* PHŒBE, *penetratingly.)*

PHŒBE *(talking nervously to keep him off the great subject).* A very sweet day indeed, sir, and the harvest being brought in. She suffers from flutterings, tremblings and spasms. But everyone is very kind and— Susan eats them all.

VALENTINE *(rises and goes to* L. *of the settee).* You coward, Miss Phœbe, to be afraid of Valentine Brown!

PHŒBE *(reproachfully).* I wrote and begged you not to come.

VALENTINE. You implied as a lover, but surely always as a friend?

PHŒBE. Oh, yes, yes!

VALENTINE *(moving above the settee).* You told Miss Livvy that you loved me once. How carefully you hid it from me!

PHŒBE. I tried to hide it from myself. *(She closes her hands together as if with something precious inside that she must not look at.)* I did not dare even look between my fingers.

VALENTINE *(speaking over her shoulder).* Until a day when your face was wet with rain.

PHŒBE. Then I thought you wanted it—and I let you— *(She cannot go on.)* Oh, I fear me it was most unladylike.

VALENTINE *(without moving).* No, but my God, it

was very ungentlemanlike. *(He pauses, then, passionately.)* Ah, ma'am, if you had but told me. *(He moves L., and down below the settee.)*

PHŒBE *(looking before her)*. A woman must never tell. You went away to the great battles; I was left to fight in a little one. Women have a flag to fly, Mr. Brown, as well as men—I tried to keep mine flying.

VALENTINE. But you ceased to care for me. *(Sitting on her L.)* I dare ask your love no more, but I still ask you to put yourself into my keeping! Miss Phœbe, let me take care of you.

PHŒBE. It cannot be.

VALENTINE. This weary teaching, let me close your school.

PHŒBE. Please, sir!

VALENTINE. If not for your own sake, I ask you, Miss Phœbe, to do it for mine. In memory of the thoughtless recruit who went off laughing to the wars. They say ladies cannot quite forget the man who has used them ill—Miss Phœbe, do it for me because I used you ill.

PHŒBE. I beg you—no more!

VALENTINE *(pause, then rising, manfully)*. There, it is all ended. Miss Phœbe, here is my hand on it. *(He gives her his hand bravely, which she presses. He rises.)*

PHŒBE. What will you do now?

VALENTINE *(crossing L.)*. I also must work. I shall become a physician again, with some drab old housekeeper to neglect me and the house. *(He turns at the fireplace.)*

PHŒBE. Oh, no.

VALENTINE. Do you foresee the cobwebs gathering and gathering in that forlorn abode?

PHŒBE. Oh, sir!

VALENTINE. You shall yet see me in Quality Street wearing my stock all awry.

PHŒBE. Oh, no!

VALENTINE *(moving a little to* R.C.*)*. With snuff upon my sleeve.

PHŒBE. Oh, no!

VALENTINE *(moving up* C., R. *of the ottoman and turning)*. No skulker, ma'am, I' hope, but gradually turning into that crusty, grumpy, bottle-nosed, not unhappy, but rather dishonoured person, an old bachelor. *(He bows.)*

PHŒBE. Oh, Mr. Brown.

VALENTINE. And all because you will not walk across the street with me.

PHŒBE. Indeed, sir. You must marry, and I hope it may be someone who is *really* like a garden.

VALENTINE. Oh. ma'am, I know but one. *(He suddenly remembers something.)* That reminds me, Miss Phœbe, of something I had forgot— (PHŒBE *rises and moves to* C. VALENTINE *produces a paper from his pocket and holds it out to her. She looks inquiringly.)* 'Tis something I have wrote about you. Read it, ma'am. 'Tis a poor trifle, I fear.

(PHŒBE *takes the paper.)*

PHŒBE *(reading it)*. "Lines to a certain lady— *(She almost breaks down.)* Who is modestly unaware of her resemblance to a garden." *(She is again moved.)* "Wrote by her servant, V. B." *(The beauty of this prevents her reading further.)*

VALENTINE *(turning up* L.C., *a little complacent over his feat)*. There is more of it, ma'am.

PHŒBE *(she is facing towards* R. *a little—reading)*.
The lilies are her pretty thoughts;
Her shoulders are the may. (oh!)
Her smiles are all forget-me-nots,
The paths her gracious way.

(She hugs the poem to her breast.)

The roses that do line it are

Her fancies walking round, ("Susan")
'Tis sweetly smelling lavender
In which my lady's gowned.

(She kisses the poem in ecstasy—goes R.C. and sits.)

VALENTINE *(excitedly, going to her)*. Miss Phœbe, when did you cease to care for me?
PHŒBE. You promised not to ask.
VALENTINE *(L. of the settee)*. I know not why you should, Miss Phœbe, but I believe you love me still.

(SUSAN *enters* L.)

SUSAN (L., *remaining near the door*). You are talking so loudly.
VALENTINE *(turning)*. Miss Susan, does she care for me still?
SUSAN *(coming* C.*)*. How could she help it?
VALENTINE. Then, by Gad, Miss Phœbe, you shall marry me, though I have to carry you in my arms to the church.
SUSAN. Phœbe, that decides it, you must marry him to avoid such a scandal. *(She sits at the settee R.C., L. end.)*
PHŒBE. I will not! I will not!
VALENTINE. I am determined to have the care of you two ladies. Miss Susan, if she will not marry me, will you? *(He sits* C.*—right of her.)*
SUSAN. Yes, I will.
VALENTINE *(triumphantly—looking at* PHŒBE*)*. Ah!
PHŒBE. Susan Throssel!
SUSAN. I cannot. I will.
PHŒBE *(fiercely)*. You, my accomplice.
VALENTINE. May I observe, Miss Phœbe, that you talk as if you were a criminal.
PHŒBE. I am! I am! As that woman! See how she shrinks. Her hands are as red as mine!

VALENTINE *(quietly)*. Is it murder? Let me see now, whom could you have murdered? Miss Livvy?

SUSAN. Phœbe, why did we not think of *that?*

(They look up, catch his eye, cower before him. VALENTINE *stares at them in turn, feeling for the first time that there is some mystery. After these glances. enter* PATTY R., *showing in* FANNY *and* HENRIETTA. VALENTINE *rises and goes up stage* C.)

PATTY. Miss Henrietta and Miss Fanny.

*(*SUSAN *rises.* HENRIETTA *and* FANNY *enter, coming to* C., *and* PATTY *exits.* HENRIETTA *curtsys to* PHŒBE *and goes* L. *to* SUSAN. FANNY *curtsys to* PHŒBE.)

HENRIETTA. I think Miss Willoughby has already popped in.

PHŒBE. Oh, yes, she has popped in several times this morning.

SUSAN. How is Miss Willoughby, Fanny? She has not been to see us for several minutes.

(She sits on the settee L.C. HENRIETTA *is on her* R.)

FANNY *(coming to* C.). Mary is so partial to you, Susan.

VALENTINE *(coming* C. *He bows,* L. *of* FANNY). You servant, Miss Henrietta—Miss Fanny.

*(They curtsy to him and sit—*FANNY L. *of* PHŒBE, HENRIETTA R. *of* SUSAN.)

FANNY. How do you do, sir?

MISS HENRIETTA. And how do you find Miss Livvy, sir?

VALENTINE. I have not seen her, Miss Henrietta.

(They exchange glances.)

HENRIETTA. Indeed!

FANNY. Not even you?

VALENTINE. You seem surprised.

FANNY. Nay, sir, you must not say so, but— *(turning to* PHŒBE*)* really, Miss Phœbe—

PHŒBE. Fanny, you presume.

VALENTINE. If one of you ladies would deign to enlighten me. To begin with, what is Miss Livvy's malady?

HENRIETTA. He does not know? Oh, Phœbe!

VALENTINE. Ladies, have pity on a dull man and explain.

FANNY. Please do not ask us to explain. 'Tis too delicate a matter. I fear I have already said more than was seemly. Phœbe, forgive!

PHŒBE. I understand, sir, there is a belief that I keep Livvy in confinement because of your passion for her.

VALENTINE *(aghast)*. My passion for Miss Livvy? Why, ma'am, I cannot abide her—nor she me. *(This causes a sensation with regard to* HENRIETTA *and* FANNY. *They are speechless.)* Furthermore, I am proud to tell you this is the lady whom I adore. *(He bows.)*

(HENRIETTA *rises.*)

FANNY. Phœbe?

VALENTINE. Yes, ma'am.

(PHŒBE *can't help enjoying her triumph, though secretly perturbed. She rises consciously with her head in the air—*SUSAN *also looking triumphant.* PHŒBE *curtsys, then goes up* R., *curtsys again and, with a little satisfied sigh, exits* R. VALENTINE *has opened the door, which he leaves open.* HENRIETTA *sits again. Both she and* FANNY *are crushed.)*

SUSAN *(rising and crossing* R.*)*. Pray excuse me for

a moment, I feel that Phœbe wants me. *(At the door.)*
Before I go I may say that I also have had an offer.

FANNY } *(together).* You!
HENRIETTA }

SUSAN. I am considering the answer.

*(She exits R., dashes up the stairs. VALENTINE bows
and closes the door. FANNY crosses and sits R. of
HENRIETTA on the settee L.C.)*

HENRIETTA. Miss Susan an offer!

FANNY. Phœbe the lady you adore! (VALENTINE
comes to C.) Sir, my felicitations—I am so happy it is
Miss Phœbe.

VALENTINE. I thank you, but can you tell me, is
there some mystery about Miss Livvy? *(Sitting on the
settee R.C., facing the ladies.)*

HENRIETTA *(eagerly).* So much so, sir, that we at
one time thought she and Miss Phœbe were the same
person.

VALENTINE. Pshaw!

FANNY. Why will they admit no physician into her
presence? The curtains are kept most tediously drawn.

HENRIETTA. And the door of the bedroom locked.

VALENTINE *(a little puzzled. He rises—looking at
the door L.).* That seems a little odd.

FANNY *(rising, excitedly crosses to the door L.).*
Henrietta, they have forgotten to remove the key.

HENRIETTA. Oh!

(They both go towards the door L.)

VALENTINE *(with a gesture of the hand).* No,
ladies.

(They are crushed.)

FANNY. No harm in knocking. *(She knocks.)* How

do you find yourself, dear Miss Livvy? *(She knocks again.)* Miss Livvy! *(She knocks again.)* Miss Livvy!
HENRIETTA. No answer.

(They cross back to L. of VALENTINE. He is at last really aroused.)

VALENTINE. I think, ladies, as a physician—

(He crosses to the door and walks into the bedroom. They are eagerly following, but he shuts the door on them. A slight pause.)

HENRIETTA *(at C.)*. We must not!
FANNY *(on her L., entreatingly)*. But—
HENRIETTA. It is the test of us as ladies.
FANNY. It is also very annoying.

(She moves down L., towards the door, holding HENRIETTA'S hand, who follows reluctantly.)

HENRIETTA. No— *(She checks FANNY and they return up L.C. VALENTINE emerges looking puzzled. He shuts the door, crosses slowly to R., watched by the ladies. Moving a little C.)* Is she so very poorly, sir?
VALENTINE *(enigmatically)*. Ah! *(He turns and goes up stage R.)*
FANNY. The case puzzles you?
VALENTINE *(coming down R.)*. It does—a little.
FANNY. Do you imply fever, sir?
VALENTINE. I would not like to say so—yet— *(He comes quickly to the door L.)*
FANNY. Poor thing! *(VALENTINE exits L.)* Henrietta, would it be ungracious to steal away now. Such amazing happenings! He loves Phœbe.
HENRIETTA. Miss Susan, an offer.
FANNY. I am as desirous to inform my sister without delay.

(VALENTINE *enters* L., *and crosses to* R.C., *as before.*)

HENRIETTA. Is it a serious malady, sir?

(VALENTINE *moves up* R.C. *and turns to them.*)

VALENTINE. I think not, but a little perplexing. With the permission of Miss Susan and Miss Phœbe I will make myself more acquainted with her disorder presently—but (*turning to the door* R.) we must not talk, lest we disturb her.

HENRIETTA. You suggest our departing, sir?

VALENTINE. Nay, ma'am, 'tis you who have suggested it. (*He bows.*)

HENRIETTA (*turning to* FANNY). I think, Fanny—

(VALENTINE *opens the door.*)

FANNY (*nodding*). Yes, Henrietta.

(HENRIETTA *crosses to the door, turns and curtsys.* FANNY *follows, curtsys, and exits after her.*)

VALENTINE (*bowing as they exit*). Ladies, your most obedient—

(*He leaves the door open and crosses to* L.C., *up stage, as* PHŒBE *enters* R.)

PHŒBE (*down* R.C., *anxiously*). Why have Miss Henietta and Fanny departed so hurriedly? (*Taking a pace* C.) They did not go in to see Livvy?

VALENTINE. No. (*He looks at her.*)

PHŒBE. Why do you look at me so strangely?

VALENTINE (*moving to the* R. *end of the settee* L.C.). Miss Phœbe, I desire to see Miss Livvy.

(SUSAN *appears in the* R. *doorway.*)

PHŒBE. Impossible. *(She crosses* L. *towards the door.)*

VALENTINE *(watching her).* Why impossible? (PHŒBE *checks at the door* L. SUSAN *is listening at the door* R.) They tell me strange stories about no one's seeing her; *(determinedly)* in short, Miss Phœbe, I will not leave this house until I have seen her.

PHŒBE *(facing front).* You cannot.

(SUSAN *enters, coming down* R.C.)

SUSAN. Phœbe, what does he want?

PHŒBE *(looking at her).* Susan—I—I— *(To* VAL-ENTINE.) Will you excuse me, sir, while I talk with Susan behind the door?

(VALENTINE *bows, as* SUSAN *crosses* L. *She turns to him there.)*

SUSAN. I particularly wish to speak to Miss Phœbe behind the door.

(She gives a little curtsy. He bows. PHŒBE *opens the door and exits, followed by* SUSAN. VALENTINE *looks after them sternly, stamps, goes* R., *changes his mind, crosses* L. *and rings the bell. He rings again. At the second ring of the bell enter* PATTY R., *wondering at bell ringing so violently.* VALENTINE *comes down* L.C., *to below the settee.)*

VALENTINE. Patty—come here—come here. (PATTY *advances to him timidly.)* Why is this trick being played upon me?

PATTY *(trying to be brazen, though alarmed).* Trick, sir? Who would dare?

VALENTINE. I know, Patty, that Miss Phœbe has been Miss Livvy all the time.

PATTY. I give in. *(Making a bolt towards* R.)

(VALENTINE *stamps and points to* C. PATTY *checks
and comes back to* C., *alarmed.*)

VALENTINE. Why has she done this?

PATTY (*anxiously*). Are you laughing, sir?

VALENTINE (*sternly*). I am very far from laughing.

PATTY (*desperate*). It was you that began it—all by
not knowing her in the white gown.

VALENTINE. But why has this deception been kept
up so long? It is infamous!

PATTY (*flaring a little*). I will not have you call her
names! (*More tenderly.*) 'Twas all playful innocence
at first, and now she is so feared of you she is weeping
her soul to death, and all I do I cannot rouse her! "I
have a follower in the kitchen, ma'am," say I to in-
furiate of her. "Give him a glass of cowslip wine," says
she, like a gentle lamb (*with a shade of reproach*) —and
ill she can afford it, you having lost all their money
for them.

VALENTINE. What is that? On the contrary, most
of the money they have, Patty, they owe to my having
invested it for them.

PATTY. That's the money they lost.

VALENTINE. You are sure of that?

PATTY. I can swear to it.

VALENTINE (*turning away to the fireplace*). Deceived me about that, also! (*He turns to face* PATTY.)
Good God, but why?

PATTY. I think she was feared you would offer to her
out of pity. She said something to Miss Susan about
keeping a flag flying. I know not what she meant.

VALENTINE. I think I know. (*He turns and leans on
the mantel.*)

PATTY (*creeping up to* L.C., *trying to see his face*).
Are you laughing, sir?

VALENTINE. No, Patty, I am not laughing. (*Turning round suddenly.*) But why do they not say Miss
Livvy has gone home? It would save them a world of
trouble.

PATTY. The Misses Willoughby and Miss Henrietta —they watch the house all day. They would say she can't be gone, for we did not see her go.

VALENTINE *(moving towards her)*. So that is it.

PATTY. And Miss Susan and Miss Phœbe wring their hands for they feared Miss Livvy is bed-ridden here for all time— (VALENTINE *laughs.* PATTY *laughs heartily also, and suddenly breaks off.)* Thank the Lord you're laughing! *(She laughs again.)*

(VALENTINE *laughs more heartily as the whole affair explains itself.* SUSAN *enters* L. PATTY *controls herself.)*

SUSAN. Why are you laughing? Are you laughing at anything in particular?

VALENTINE. No, only at things in general.

SUSAN. I am happy to inform you, sir, that Miss Livvy finds herself much improved.

(VALENTINE *bows grandly.* PATTY *is alarmed.)*

VALENTINE. It is joy to me to hear it.

SUSAN. She is coming in to see you.

PATTY. Oh, but, ma'am—

(Exit SUSAN L.*)*

VALENTINE. Go away Patty.

PATTY. But—

VALENTINE. Anon, I may claim a service of you, but for the present go—

PATTY. But—but—

VALENTINE *(dramatically)*. Retire, woman. (PATTY *bursts into laughter and exits* R., *leaving the door open.* VALENTINE *goes to the window, peeps through the curtains, chuckling. Enter* PHŒBE L., *without cap, her ringlets hanging. She wears a dressing-gown, suggesting that she has risen from bed and has the manner of an*

invalid. She is leaning on SUSAN. VALENTINE *comes
down* R. *of the settee to* L.C. *The ladies retire a step.
Mock sympathetically.)* Oh! but how sad, how very sad.
Your servant, Miss Livvy.

PHŒBE *(weakly).* How do you do, sir?

VALENTINE *(very solemnly).* Allow me, Miss Susan.
(He goes to help her.)

PHŒBE *(bravely).* No, no—I—I can walk alone—
see.

(She goes to the settee L.C., *while he solicitously arranges the cushions at the* R. *end. She reclines her
head. He is behind her, and* SUSAN *stands at the* L.
end.)

VALENTINE. Bravo! Excellent! Splendid, Miss
Livvy—

SUSAN. How do you think she is looking?

VALENTINE *(who has assumed a very professional
air).* Pale—decidedly pulled down. Excuse me, Miss
Livvy. *(He puts a hand on her forehead, pulls up one
eyelid, and feels her pulse.)* Umph! Aha! Oh, oh, oh!

SUSAN. What do you think?

VALENTINE. She will recover. *(Suddenly.)* May I
say, ma'am, it surprises me that anyone should see
much resemblance between Miss Livvy and her aunt
Phœbe. Miss Phœbe is decidedly shorter and more
thick-set.

PHŒBE *(sitting up, indignantly).* Oh, no, I'm not.

VALENTINE. I said Miss Phœbe, ma'am. (PHŒBE,
recollecting, dives into the pillow again.) But tell me,
is not Miss Phœbe to join us?

PHŒBE. She hopes you will excuse her, sir.

SUSAN. Taking the opportunity of airing the room.

VALENTINE. Ah, very wise, very wise.

SUSAN *(going down to the door* L., *she opens it and
calls).* Captain Brown will excuse you, Phœbe.

VALENTINE *(coming down* L.C., *calling).* Certainly,
Miss Phœbe. Continue to air the room. (SUSAN *shuts*

the door. VALENTINE *suddenly goes to* PHŒBE, *peers into her face. She shrinks away a little. Crossing to* R.C.) Well, ma'am, I think I could cure Miss Livvy, if she is put unreservedly into my hands.

SUSAN *(at* L. *of the settee).* I am sure you could.

VALENTINE *(turning).* Then you are my patient, Miss Livvy.

PHŒBE *(sitting up).* 'Twas but a passing indisposition, sir—I am almost quite recovered. *(She moves to the* L. *end of the settee.)*

VALENTINE. Nay, you still require attention. *(Sitting beside her,* R. *of her, he jerks her face round to him.)* Do you propose making a long stay in Quality Street?

(SUSAN *sits in the chair* L.)

PHŒBE. I—I—I— It—it depends.

SUSAN. Mary is the worst!

VALENTINE. I ask your pardon.

PHŒBE. Aunt Susan, you are excited.

VALENTINE. But you are quite right, Miss Livvy, home is the place for you.

PHŒBE. Would that I could go there!

(SUSAN *throws up her hands.)*

VALENTINE. You are going.

PHŒBE *(a little taken aback).* Yes—soon.

VALENTINE *(blandly, as if a doctor to a child—a manner he keeps up).* Indeed I have a delightful surprise for you, Miss Livvy—you are going to-day.

PHŒBE. To-day?

VALENTINE *(genially).* Yes, to-day. (SUSAN *leans anxiously towards them. As if expecting her to be delighted.)* And not merely to-day, but now.

PHŒBE. Now! *(She exchanges a quick glance of perturbation with* SUSAN.)

VALENTINE. As it happens my carriage is standing idle at your door, and I am to take you in it to your home. How happy will my old friend James Throssel be to see his daughter once again.

(The glance, repeated. is a guilty one. PHŒBE *gives a little gasp.)*

PHŒBE *(breathlessly).* You take me?
VALENTINE *(genially).* Nay, it is no trouble at all. Miss Susan, some wraps for her. *(He rises and moves a little down .)*
SUSAN *(rising).* But—but—
PHŒBE. Sir, I decline to go.
VALENTINE *(turning).* Come, Miss Livvy, you are in my hands.
PHŒBE. I decline, I am most determined.
VALENTINE. You admit yourself that you are recovered.
PHŒBE *(quickly).* I don't feel quite so well now. Aunt Susan— (SUSAN *goes to her.)* —another of those spasms.

(She "acts" a spasm. reclining on SUSAN, *who has sat on her* L.)

VALENTINE. Yes, yes—a very good sign.

*(*SUSAN *makes to rise.)*

PHŒBE. Auntie, don't leave me.
VALENTINE. What a refractory patient it is. *(To their consternation he crosses* L.) But humour her, Miss Susan, and I shall ask Miss Phœbe for the wraps.

(He exits L. PHŒBE *squeals and springs up, going to* C. SUSAN *stares at the door* L. PHŒBE, *after one frightened glance* L., *turns and runs off* R.)

SUSAN *(running after her).* Phœbe, do not leave me— *(She checks* R.C., *hearing* VALENTINE *returning.)*

(Re-enter VALENTINE L., *carrying heavy wraps.* SUSAN
stands amazed.)

VALENTINE *(from the door, genially).* I think these
will do admirably, Miss Susan. You can send her trunks
after her.

SUSAN *(staggered).* But Phœbe—

VALENTINE. If I swathe Miss Livvy in these.

SUSAN. Phœbe! *(She comes to* C.*)*

VALENTINE. She is still occupied in airing the room.

SUSAN. What? *(She retreats a pace up* C.*)*

VALENTINE *(going to the settee* L.C.. *arranging the
wraps on it).* Come, Miss Livvy, put these over you.
Allow me—there—this one over your shoulders, so.
Be so obliging as to lean on me. Come now, then—yes,
yes. Now be brave, you cannot fall. *(Going towards*
R.*)* My arm is round you, that's a good girl—gently,
gently, Miss Livvy, hold your head up. *(He throws
the hood up.)* Ah, that's it—we are doing famously—
come—come. *(He turns at* R.C.*)* Miss Susan, your most
obedient. I will take every care of her. Come along,
Miss Livvy. *(Going out.)* I'll put you in my carriage.

(He exits R., *as if supporting her, leaving* SUSAN *who,
watching this uncanny business, has crept down* C.,
aghast. The door off R. *is heard to slam.* SUSAN *collapses on the settee at* R.C. *She sits staring straight
before her. Enter* PHŒBE R., *running. She closes
the door, quaking; she has put her hair under a cap
again.)*

PHŒBE *(coming down* C.*).* He is gone. *(Sighing re-
lief. She sees* SUSAN'S *strange face.)* Oh, Susan, was
he as dreadful as that?

SUSAN *(looking before her, in an unnatural tone).*
Phœbe, he knows all.

PHŒBE. Oh, of course he knows all now. *(Moving
to* L. *of the settee.)* Sister, sister, did his face change?
Oh, Susan, what did he say?

SUSAN *(still gazing before her)*. He said, "Your most obedient." That was almost all he said.

PHŒBE. Did his eyes flash fire?

SUSAN. Phœbe, it was what he did. He—he took Livvy with him.

PHŒBE *(backing to R., fearing SUSAN's distress has unhinged her brain)*. Susan dear, don't say that. You are not distraught, are you?

SUSAN *(sepulchrally)*. He did—he wrapped her up in a cloak.

(PHŒBE's fears are confirmed. She comes to SUSAN and kneels, on her L., patting her hands.)

PHŒBE. Susan! You are Susan Throssel, my love. You remember me, don't you? Phœbe, your sister. I was, Livvy also—you know—Livvy.

SUSAN. He took Livvy with him.

PHŒBE *(in agony)*. Oh, oh! Sister, who am I?

SUSAN. You are Phœbe.

PHŒBE. And who was Livvy?

SUSAN. You were.

PHŒBE *(rising)*. Thank heaven.

SUSAN. But he took her away in the carriage.

PHŒBE. Oh, dear! *(She comes behind her.)* Susan, you will soon be well again. Let us occupy our minds. Shall we draw up the advertisement for the re-opening of the school?

SUSAN. I do so hate the school.

PHŒBE *(moving down R. of the settee)*. Come, dear, come.

SUSAN *(rising)*. No.

PHŒBE *(leading SUSAN across to the bureau R.)*. Yes, dear, come along—sit down and write. *(She seats SUSAN at the bureau with pen, ink, paper, and puts a quill into her hand.)* Write, Susan.

SUSAN. Ugh! *(She shudders.)*

PHŒBE *(standing behind her, dictates)*. "The Misses Throssel have the pleasure to announce—

SUSAN. Pleasure! Oh, Phœbe! *(She writes.)*

PHŒBE *(looking before her and speaking determinedly, and bravely).* —that they will resume school on the *(pause for thought)* fifth of next month. Music, embroidery, the backboard and all elegancies of the mind, orthography—"

SUSAN. How do you spell it?

PHŒBE. The printers are so clever at that "Latin."

SUSAN. Latin?

PHŒBE *(sternly).* "Latin." Shall we say algebra?

SUSAN. I refuse to write algebra.

PHŒBE *(quaking).* "For beginners—"

SUSAN. I refuse! *(She flings down the quill and rises.)* There is but one thing I can write—it writes itself in my head all day. *(Crossing to* L.C. *with the paper in her hand.)* "Miss Susan Throssel presents her compliments to the Misses Willoughby and Miss Henrietta Turnbull and request the honour of their presence at the nuptials of her sister, Phœbe, and Captain Valentine Brown."

PHŒBE *(running to her).* Susan!

SUSAN *(turning).* Phœbe! *(Her arms outstretched to* PHŒBE. *They break down, embracing, at* C. *The door slam is heard off* R. *Disengaging.)* He has returned!

PHŒBE. Oh, cruel, cruel! *(Clutching* SUSAN.*)* Susan, I am alarmed.

*(*SUSAN *releases herself.* PHŒBE *backs a pace up* C.*)*

SUSAN. I shall face him. *(Crossing* R.C.*)* I am a lion at bay. Oh! *(She turns and returns to* L.C.*)*

PHŒBE *(coming down* R. *of* SUSAN, *and assuming an attitude of defiance).* Nay, if one of us must face him, I will!

*(*SUSAN *hides behind her. Enter* VALENTINE R. PHŒBE *turns up to the* R. *end of the settee* L.C.*)*

VALENTINE *(bowing and coming to* R.C.*)* Miss Livvy will never trouble you any more, Miss Susan. I have sent her home.

SUSAN *(going* L.*)*. Oh, sir, how can you invent such a story for us?

VALENTINE. I did not. (SUSAN *turns to face him.*) I invented it for the Misses Willoughby and Miss Henrietta. *(Going up* R.C. *he bows to the window.)* They watched me pack her into my carriage. *(Returning down* R.C.*)* Patty accompanied her and in a few hours Patty will return alone.

SUSAN. Phœbe, he has got rid of Livvy. *(She sinks into the stool down* L.*)*

PHŒBE. Susan, his face has not changed.

VALENTINE *(moving to* PHŒBE*)*. Miss Phœbe, it is not raining, but your face is wet. I wish always to kiss you when your face is wet. *(He kisses her.)*

PHŒBE. Susan!

VALENTINE. Dear Phœbe Throssel, will you be Phœbe Brown?

PHŒBE. But you know everything, and that I am not a garden.

VALENTINE. I know everything, ma'am, except that. Miss Phœbe, will you?

SUSAN *(entreatingly)*. Oh, yes. *(She hides her face timidly.)*

(PHŒBE *looks at* SUSAN *deprecatingly; then quietly prim, gives* VALENTINE *her hand.)*

PHŒBE. Sir, the dictates of my heart enjoin me to accept your too flatterng offer. *(She gives a very formal curtsy.* VALENTINE *kisses her hand, takes her cap off and lets the ringlets fall once more, kisses the cap and puts it in his breast-pocket, puts her on the settee at the fireplace and kisses her on the lips.* SUSAN *rises, tears up the paper, and is turning down* L. *Pointing.)* Oh, sir, Susan also.

(VALENTINE *crosses to* SUSAN, *brings her to the settee, kisses her, and she sits with a sigh of pleasure on the settee, as he also sits, between them and turns to look at* PHŒBE.)

CURTAIN.

QUALITY STREET

FURNITURE AND PROPERTY PLOT

ACT ONE

(NOTE.—*It is important that the general colour scheme of the décor should be in blue and white. This applies to the curtains, furniture coverings, cushions, etc., and also to book covers and other details. The walls should be in these colours also. If possible the carpet should be blue, or at least have blue as the basic colour of its design.*)

Carpet on the stage.

On the walls, some delicate water colours and/or etchings.

Casement curtains at the bay window (blue, or blue and white).

Heavier blue curtains to draw across the bay.

Mantelpiece over the fire (L.) in white and blue.

> *On the Mantel.*—Clock.
>
> Ornaments.
>
> A strutted mirror (round if possible).

Fender and fireirons. Hob on the grate.

A black glove hanging above the fire.

2 settees, R.C. and L.C.. as shown on the Ground Plan.

> (The one at R.C. is of the type known as a "duet stool." The other should be wood framed, though it is referred to as an "ottoman." They are upholstered in blue and the covers are attached to the legs with dainty bows to which reference is made.)

> *On the Settees.*—Cushions.
>
> Coverlets draped over the back or the arms.

2 chairs, with arms (one L. of the settee L.C.; one up R.).

A square stool (down L., for FANNY).

A spinet, with a music-stool below it.

On the Spinet.—Music.

A bowl of flowers.

A large bureau. The upper part having leaded glass doors. The lower part having one or two drawers. A writing shelf above the drawers, opened out when required, with writing materials.

A wedding dress in one drawer.

Small oblong table up L., with decanter and 3 wine-glasses.

Small round table above the fire (used for tea, and to set a lamp when required).

Large sheet of paper on the table.

Work basket (R. of the bay).

Tea caddy (casket type) on the low stand down R.

Embroidered screen, on a stand.

Low plant stand, with plant.

PERSONAL.

FANNY.—Book, small handkerchief.

MISS WILLOUGHBY ⎫ Small dainty handkerchiefs,
HENRIETTA.   ⎬ knitting and reticules for
SUSAN.   ⎭ the same.

PHŒBE.—Pattens, muff (first entrance).

PATTY. (off R.).—Tea-tray, with silver tea-set, cups and saucers for two.

(For later entrance.) Plate of cakes.

VALENTINE.—Hat, stick, gloves.

EFFECTS.

Snow.

Clock chime (four).

Door creak (down L.).

Door slam (off R.).

ACT TWO

Strike all furniture *except:*
>Settee L.C. (set a little further up stage).
>Spinet and music-stool.
>Small table.
>Bureau.
>Curtains. (These may be changed to duller ones if circumstances permit.)

Carpet covered with plain stage cloth.
>*Set:*
>High desk, as used in a school. Stool behind it.
>Short form to L. of the desk.
>2 long forms. (One set up L.C., parallel to the floats. The other to the L., diagonally, end pointing down L.)
>2 "globes." (One, large, down R. ; the other, small, on the spinet.)
>*On the Walls.*—In place of the pictures, several large maps.
>*On the Desk.*—Several books, papers, ink, quills, chalks.
>*On the Small Table.*—A cane.

Personal.

ARTHUR.—Dunce's cap.
CHILDREN.—Books, satchels, etc.
PHŒBE (off R.).—Lighted candle, on candlestick.
VALENTINE.—Phial, wrapped in paper.
LAMPLIGHTER.—Torch, steps.

Effects.

Band off stage.

ACT THREE

Stage covered with "grass." A matting strip at each long seat.

Coloured lanterns hung, or candles in fittings attached
   to tent supports.
4 card tables (see Ground Plan).
4 chairs at each table, or stools.
   (Note.—The seat below the table down L.C. must be
   a stool, or short "rout seat.")
A couch at C.
A couch, or long "rout seat," against the L. wall of the
   tent pavilion.

PERSONAL.

LADIES.—Feather fans (HARRIET'S fan to have one or
   two feathers loose enough to be drawn easily).
BLADES (off R.).—A glass of brandy.
   (Note.—PHŒBE'S *cloak to be on the* C. *couch at the
   rise of the* CURTAIN.)

EFFECTS.

Talking crowd off stage.
Band off stage (dance music of the period).

ACT FOUR

Carpet, walls and furniture as for Act I.
The settee L.C. is moved down to Act I position.
The chair L. is turned towards the fire slightly.
The flowers are changed. The small round table is
   moved from up L. to above the settee L.C.
   (Note.—*Writing materials in bureau desk for this
   Act.)*

PERSONAL.

MISS WILLOUGHBY.—Bowl of "arrowroot," covered
   with a napkin.

Susan.—Spoon for the above (off down L.).
Valentine.—Sheet of notepaper (verses).
     Wraps and hooded cloak for "Miss Livvy" (off
     stage, down L.).
Phœbe.—Additional cap (off stage R.).

QUALITY STREET

LIGHTING PLOT

ACT ONE

To Open.—Floats: Amber, pink and blue, all at ½.
Battens (over interior): Amber, pink, blue, all at ¾.
Batten over exterior: Amber FULL, blue ¾.
Stage flood on exterior cloth: Steel. frost.
Ground row on cloth: Amber and blue ½.
F.O.H.: Steel (frost) ½, No. 7 pink (frost) ½.
Amber lengths on interior backings.

Cue 1.—PHŒBE. "Susan, you have been talking to them about V. B."— Slow check of amber in floats and battens by ¼; check down steel F.O.H.

Cue 2.—*As* PATTY *brings in the tea*—Commence slow change of flood on cloth from steel to No. 18 blue (frost); check No. 4 batten, amber, by ¼. Bring up pink in floats and No. 1 batten only, very slightly. Continue to check steel F.O.H.

Cue 3.—PHŒBE. "Nay, sir, you must not ask me that."—Commence slow check of amber in floats and battens by ¼. At the same time bring pink and blue up by ⅛. Fade amber in No. 4 batten and ground row, to *nil*. Slow change of steel F.O.H. to No. 52 gold (frost) at ½ (completed at exit of VALENTINE).

Snow effects as indicated in the script.

ACT TWO

To Open.—Floats: Amber and pink ½, white and blue ¼.

Battens (over interior): Amber and pink ¾, white and blue ¼.

No. 4 Batten (over exterior): Amber FULL, white ½, blue ½.

Stage flood on exterior cloth: Straw (frost).

Ground row on cloth: Amber ½, white ¼.

F.O.H. flood No. 52 gold (frost) and No. 7 pink (frost).

Amber lengths on interior backings.

Cue 1.—SUSAN. "Indeed. sir, I think you are monstrous fine."—Commence slow check (10 minutes) of amber and white in floats to *nil.*

Ditto of the interior battens, amber to ¼, white to *nil,* pink to ½.

Ditto No. 4 batten, amber to ½, white to *nil.*

Slowly change flood on cloth to No. 18 blue (frost) at ½.

White in ground row *nil,* amber ¼.

F.O.H.—10 minutes to fade OUT.

Cue 2.—*As* LAMPLIGHTER *disappears off* R.—Bring in No 52 gold spot over R. acting area in street.

Cue 3.—*As* PATTY *turns up the lamp on the table up* L.C.—Bring in batten spot. No. 52 gold, over L. acting area. At the same time, bring in L. section *only,* of amber in floats to ¼, ditto No. 1 batten, amber ½.

ACT THREE

To Open.—Floats: Amber, pink and blue ½.

Battens (over tent interior): Amber, pink, blue ¾.

Batten over exterior: Blue FULL, pink ½.

Ground rows: Blue and pink ¼.

Stage flood: Moonlight blue (frost) at ¼, off up L. to flood exterior cloth and L. backing. very softly.

(Interior of tent pavilion to have candles, or coloured lanterns. If desired, batten spots may
replace the floats and battens described above,
to spot acting areas, No. 52 gold, using with
them pink and blue floats at $\frac{1}{4}$.)

No Cues.

ACT FOUR

To Open.—Lighting as for Act **II.**
No Cues.

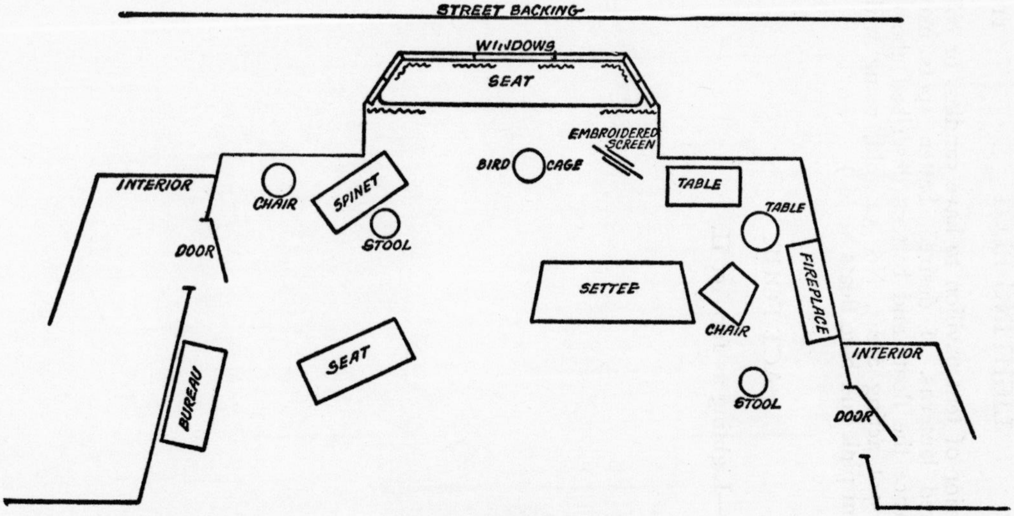
STREET BACKING
WINDOWS
SEAT
EMBROIDERED SCREEN
BIRD CAGE
INTERIOR
CHAIR
SPINET
STOOL
DOOR
TABLE
TABLE
SETTEE
CHAIR
FIREPLACE
SEAT
BUREAU
INTERIOR
STOOL
DOOR

SCENE DESIGN - ACT I
"QUALITY STREET"

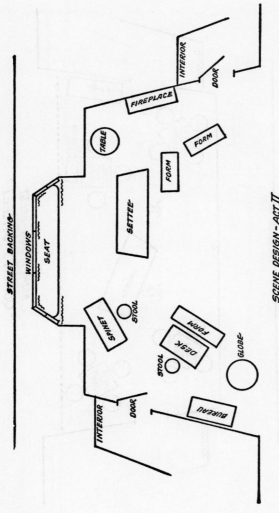

SCENE DESIGN - ACT II
"QUALITY STREET"

SCENE DESIGN—ACT III
"QUALITY STREET"

DEAR PHOEBE

Comedy. 3 acts. By Tom Taggart and James Reach.
Adapted from the famous television series "Dear Phoebe,"
based on characters created by Alex Gottlieb and starring
Peter Lawford.
6 men, 7 women. Interior.

This riotous and explosive comedy is concerned with the hectic events that take place in the editorial offices of the *Daily Star*. Bill Hastings, a likable young college teacher, decides to become a newspaper man. After many tribulations, he finally gets in to see the Managing Editor, the redoubtable and irascible G. R. Fosdick. Bill does get taken on—taken on as "Aunt Phoebe Goodheart," dispenser of advice to the lovelorn! Bill falls hard for Mickey Riley, only female sports editor in captivity. Impetus for the hilarious, madcap complications that ensue is provided by a letter that arrives for Aunt Phoebe from Rochelle Mignonne. Rochelle has evidence implicating night club owner Big Joe Moroni in a sports-fix scandal, and Bill, with Mickey's help, goes after the story. To do so, he has to dress up as "Aunt Phoebe"—and then things really start popping. Almost under the noses of Bill and Mickey, Rochelle is murdered, and they have to solve her killing before the next morning's deadline. (Royalty, $35-$25.) Price, $1.25.

DRAGNET*

*REG. U.S. PAT. OFF. © SHERRY TV, INC.
Play. 3 acts. By James Reach.
5 men, 5 women. Interior. (Unit set.)

Adaptation of one of the most famous radio and television programs. Taken from the files of the Los Angeles Police Department, the case in the play is that of a supposed suicide, Karl Hamlin. Sergeant Friday and his partner, Officer Frank Smith, working out of Homicide, are called to the home of Hamlin's estranged wife, Nora. There they are informed that Hamlin has locked himself in the study and shot himself. The detectives are forced to smash a window to gain entrance to the study, where they find Hamlin dead and, clutched in his hand, a revolver from which one shot has recently been fired. On the surface, it looks like a routine case. But—a laboratory check proves conclusively that the fatal bullet could not have been fired from the revolver, and Friday and Smith are confronted with a seemingly insoluble problem. Through a brilliant feat of detection, Friday is able to unmask the killer in a stunning and totally unexpected climax, and justice is served.
(Royalty, $35-$25.) Price, $1.25.

COME SHARE MY CLOUD (BIBI)

Comedy. 3 acts. By Paul S. Nathan.

4 males, 4 females. One set, Interior-Patio.

Bibi is an imaginative, motherless girl on the threshold of adolescence. When a handsome stranger wanders by mistake into her room just off the garden, Bibi weaves him into a romantic fairy tale. Ali Reza Khosrovani is with the Iranian delegation to the United Nations. Charmed by Bibi and touched by her courage in the face of an approaching operation, "Al" offers her the warm supporting relationship her family are too busy to provide. Aunt Mary and sister Zelda, meeting Al, find him just as attractive as Bibi does, but are shocked to discover that she thinks he is planning to marry her a few years hence. They realize she has turned to him for affection which normally should come from her world-traveling father. Al is even more upset at his predicament—particularly since he has lost his heart to Aunt Mary. After the operation is over and Bibi is strong enough, she is told the shattering truth. Luckily, her father has arrived at a belated recognition of his responsibility toward Bibi, as well as his own need for her love, and is on hand to cushion the blow.

(Royalty, $25-$20.) Price, $1.25.

THE BROOM AND THE GROOM

Comedy. 3 acts. By Kurtz Gordon and Robert Emmett

4 males, 6 females. Simple unit set.

David Thompson, greatly disturbed because his young bride, Alma, professes to be a witch, challenged Alma to prove it. Unfortunately the challenge is made on the Eve of Halloween. Alma's aunt Rina arrives from Boston to perpetuate a ritual for the new bride. She bears two important gifts—a witch cake and an old, long-strawed broom that has been in the family for generations. When the broom is presented to Alma, David, fed up with it all, grabs it and tears off the wrapping. He is answered by sudden thunder, wind and rain. Alma, faced with an emergency of transportation, resorts to the broom. Her flight is picked up by radar, and the Air Corps is alerted. David, beside himself, calls on Aunt Rina for assistance. The surprise ending puts David's world back in its proper orbit.

(Royalty, $25-$20.) Price, $1.25.

EIGHTEENTH SUMMER

Comedy. 3 acts. By Bernice Martin.

6 males, 6 females. Exterior (Patio)

Life becomes complicated for Molly when her cousin, Jeannine, becomes her houseguest for the summer. Jeannine confides to Molly that she is recently married, and that her father has sent her to stay with Molly's family in the hope that a wholesome life with a normal small-town family will cure her of what Father considers an ill-advised marriage. Jeannine breaks up the love affair between Molly's best friend, Judy, and Duncan, with whom Molly herself is secretly but hopelessly in love. Jeannine is instrumental in involving Duncan, and Sandy, who is staying with the Duncans, in a hit-and-run accident. Sandy's intelligent manner of handling the crisis brought on by Jeannine's lack of principle makes Molly begin to see the people around her in a more realistic perspective. Molly wrestles with conflicting loyalties and the drawing knowledge that assuming adult responsibilities is a more complicated business than she had realized.

(Royalty, $25-$20.) Price, $1.25.

PETEY'S CHOICE

Comedy. 3 acts. By Fred Carmichael.

4 males, 5 females, 3 walk-ons. Interior.

The play revolves around the Lansing family and shows the way a man's family saves him from compromising his principles. Peter Lansing's past catches up to him when a recording he made as "Petey" Lansing 15 years ago suddenly becomes Number One on the Hit Parade. Peter is about to be appointed president of the college where he teaches when he is catapulted into the public eye and becomes the newest rage. When he is almost coerced into accepting the presidency under terms of the conservative Board of Trustees, his wife and two daughters take a desperate gamble for him behind his back. The lines are funny and the situations uproarious, but underneath lies the lesson that education should be modernized and teaching methods adapted to the student of today.

(Royalty, $25-$20.) Price, $1.25.

YOU, THE JURY

Courtroom drama. 3 acts. By James Reach.

7 males, 8 females. Interior.

Presents an ingenious and completely novel idea in permitting the audience as a whole to act as a jury and vote whether Barbara Scott—on trial for the murder of Chester Arthur Brand —is innocent or guilty. Extremely simple in its production and setting. The cause of Barbara Scott, defended by her attractive lawyer-sister Edith, and prosecuted by the dynamic young Allan Woodward, seems hopeless at the outset. Step by step, Allan relentlessly builds up the case against her—including her purported confession of guilt, and culminating in the dramatic testimony of Brant's fiancee, Sheila Vincent, who claims she saw Barbara in almost the very act of firing the fatal shot. But Edith Scott refuses to give up; doggedly she keeps fighting back on behalf of her sister, and she is finally rewarded when help arrives from a totally unexpected source. The action keeps driving forward, building in conflict and in tension—until the stirring climax is reached, and the audience—*You, the Jury*— renders its verdict!

(Royalty, $25-$20.) Price, $1.25.

THE MAN ON A STICK

Comedy. 3 acts. By Leon Ware and Harlan Ware.

5 males, 4 females. Interior.

This is the story of the warm-hearted, lovable, much-put-upon Burton Travener who, at the insistence of his employer, reads a self-help book about positive thinking called *The Dominant Male*—and belatedly tries to become one in his house of cards. His second wife, Mildred, her mother, Mrs. Sophie Newcomb, and their old friend, the jaunty, unscrupulous Frank Egan contribute to the collapse of the household Burton has tried to maintain for his daughter Janie whose poignant love story is interwoven through the engrossing tale. Two neighbors, the ancient Judge Randall Corp, and a nine-year-old Cub Scout, Edgar Beecham, provide a rescue in comic and exciting terms in Burton's darkest hour. "One of the most popular plays in the history of the Pasadena Playhouse."—*Gilmore Brown*.

(Royalty, $25-$20.) Price, $1.25.

PAPA IS ALL

Comedy. 3 acts. By Patterson Greene. 3 males, 3 females. Interior. Modern costumes.

Papa Is All, first produced at the Guild Theatre in New York, is a cheerful comedy about the Pennsylvania Dutch. Papa is a tyrant, club-footed, ugly tempered. Emma, the daughter, is in love with a surveyor who wants to marry her. The son, Jake, wants to simplify farm life by the installation of machinery. Mama is wistful for the friendly association with neighbors that is a normal part of even the most orthodox Mennonite life. Emma precipitates a crises by stealing away to attend a picture show in Lancaster in the company of her young surveyor. A neighbor inadvertently reveals Emma's secret, and Papa sweeps off in a rage to shoot the pleasant young man. Apparently the gods are on the family's side. The car in which Papa is riding to his shooting is fortunately wrecked at a railroad crossing and Pappa happily disappears. What his fate is, and how finally Papa is really done in, unfolds in the third act. "A light and completely entertaining play . . . popular comedy with a funny plot and a background of Mennonite manners . . . well-bred lark in folksy style."—*New York Times.* Excellent comedy for Little Theatres and colleges.

(Royalty, $35.00.)

NO TIME FOR COMEDY

Comedy. 3 acts. By S. N. Behrman. 4 males, 3 females. 2 interiors. Modern costumes.

First produced by Katharine Cornell and the Playwright's Company in New York with Katharine Cornell and Laurence Olivier in the leading roles. Gaylord Easterbrook is a clever young playwright whose comedies are highly successful. He is married to Linda, a brilliant actress who stars in all his plays. But Gay is discontented and restless, and he feels that the modern tempo and constant change demand reality and a serious approach. He is encouraged in this opinion by Amanda Smith, a restless dabbler and society woman. With her as an inspiration Gay manages to write a serious play about death and the Spanish Loyalists. Through all this apparent affair Linda carefully walks, and of course, comes out the undisputed winner when it is obvious that Gay is not going to elope with Amanda, who wants to run away. "Another 'must' on the play-going curriculum."— N. Y. *Journal-American.* "*No Time For Comedy* is a dainty, amusing delight."—N. Y. *Times.*

(Royalty, $35.00.)

OLD ACQUAINTANCE

Comedy, 3 acts. By John van Druten. 2 males, 5 females. 2 interiors. Modern costumes.

This gentle, sincere and understanding comedy was first produced in New York City by Dwight Deere Wiman with Peggy Wood and Jane Cowl in the leading roles. A great popular as well as critical success. Katherine Markhom is a brilliant American novelist whose works are admired by many but bought by few. Her oldest friend is Mildred Watson Drake, whose popular novels have made her a rich woman. Katherine has quite a satisfaitory attachment with Rudd, a man some ten years her junior, and she has just about decided to marry him. But Rudd, somewhat to his own surprise, falls desperately in love with Deirdre Drake, Mildred's daughter. It is then necessary for Katherine and Mildred to go through the business of discussing the situation in what is most certainly a scintillating fashion. It is rather to the astonishment of all concerned that the attachment of the younger people leads to a greater understanding between the women and serves to cement their friendship where it was thought it might have permanently disrupted it. This is highly recommended for advanced amateurs. "A trenchant, clever, and sophisticated comedy."—Robert Coleman, *Daily Mirror*.

(Royalty, $35.00.)

YES AND NO

Play. 2 acts and epilogue. By Kenneth Horne. 3 males, 4 females. Interior. Modern costumes.

We went all the way to England to find an answer to that ever recurring question: Have you anything that's different? "Yes and No" *is* different. Judge for yourself from these few lines taken from the London Ambassador's Theatre program: The action of Act I takes place on Wednesday and Thursday and shows what might have happened if Jo had said "No." The action of Act II takes place on the same two days, showing what might have happened if Jo had said "Yes." The Epilogue reverts again to Wednesday and shows what actually happened. But the plot isn't the only remarkable thing in this pleasant little comedy. It's the characters who matter: seven of the most genial, the most refreshing, the most amusing fuddie-duddies people this play as have ever walked upon a stage. We recommend it without a single reservation for High School or Little Theatre production.

(Royalty, $25.00.)